Achmat Dangor

KAFKA'S CURSE

VINTAGE INTERNATIONAL

Vintage Books

A Division of Random House, Inc.

New York

FIRST VINTAGE INTERNATIONAL EDITION, MARCH 2000

Copyright © 1997 by Achmat Dangor

The Library of Congress has cataloged the Pantheon edition as follows:

Dangor, Achmat, 1948—
Kafka's curse / Achmat Dangor.
p. cm.
ISBN 0-375-40510-0
1. East Indians—South Africa—Fiction.
2. Muslims—South Africa—Fiction.
3. Jews—South Africa—Fiction. I. Title.
PR9369.3.D26K33 1999
98-27866
CIP
823—dc21

Vintage ISBN: 0-375-70462-0

Author photograph © Annari Van Der Merwe

www.vintagebooks.com

Printed in the United States of America
10   9   8   7   6   5   4   3   2   1

Achmat Dangor

KAFKA'S CURSE

Achmat Dangor was born in Johannesburg in 1948, the year the Nationalist Party, the architects of apartheid, won power in South Africa. Winner of many literary prizes, including the 1998 Charles Herman Bosman prize for *Kafka's Curse*, he is the author of three collections of poetry, a novella and short story collection, and a novel. This is his first book to be published in the United States. He lives in South Africa.

INTERNATIONAL

KAFKA'S CURSE

FOR AUDREY

. . . after that long kiss I near lost my breath yes he said I was a flower of the mountain yes so we are flowers all a womans body yes that was one true thing he said in his life . . .

JAMES JOYCE, Ulysses

DESCENDANTS
OF PATRICK WALLACE

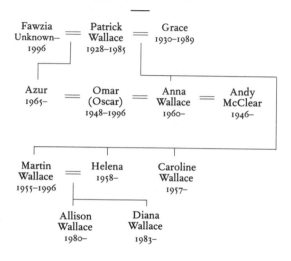

Fawzia Unknown–1996 = Patrick Wallace 1928–1985 = Grace 1930–1989

Azur 1965– = Omar (Oscar) 1948–1996 = Anna Wallace 1960– = Andy McClear 1946–

Martin Wallace 1955–1996 = Helena 1958– Caroline Wallace 1957–

Allison Wallace 1980– Diana Wallace 1983–

DESCENDANTS
OF SALIM
—

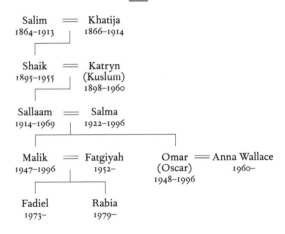

Salim
1864–1913
═
Khatija
1866–1914

Shaik
1895–1955
═
Katryn
(Kuslum)
1898–1960

Sallaam
1914–1969
═
Salma
1922–1996

Malik
1947–1996
═
Fatgiyah
1952–

Omar
(Oscar)
1948–1996
═
Anna Wallace
1960–

Fadiel
1973–

Rabia
1979–

DESCENDANTS
OF EBRAHIM
(ABE) SCHROEDER
—

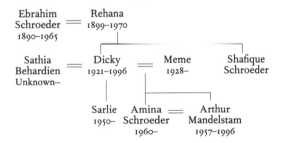

Ebrahim
Schroeder
1890–1965
═
Rehana
1899–1970

Sathia
Behardien
Unknown–
═
Dicky
1921–1996
═
Meme
1928–

Shafique
Schroeder

Sarlie
1950–

Amina
Schroeder
1960–
═
Arthur
Mandelstam
1957–1996

KAFKA'S CURSE

Moving to the Suburbs

IN THE END, Anna left her husband Oscar
because he breathed down her neck. At first his
breathing had been his most endearing quality.
Through many years of unconscious practice,
Oscar had developed the perfect breathing tech
nique: breath in through the nose, breath out
through the mouth. He did this with such serenity that he seemed to Anna the most sensitive and
refined man she had known. Even more so than
her father. She loved Oscar for his gentleness,
his ability to smile when affronted, his understanding of her need to rage at life's many and
inevitable little agonies. Even when he was the
cause and object of Anna's anger. Oscar's strength
lay in his reticence: the hesitancy that in others
seemed like a vice or a weakness became in Oscar
a thoughtful virtue. All of this Anna attributed to

Oscar's capacity to fill his lungs with invigorating oxygen, his finely structured, somewhat hooked nose quivering like that of a thoroughbred horse.

Then Oscar was struck by an illness that reversed the whole natural order of his being. It began with a headache which the doctor put down to an infection in his sinus cavity. At first his breathing acquired a hoarseness associated with chest colds or the flu and did not unduly disturb their bedtime tranquillity. But gradually Oscar's condition worsened, his breathing became irregular and his struggling lungs began to make harsh, anguished noises. Suddenly he was overcome, each night, by coughing spasms that shook his body, his eyes bulging as if he were near to madness. Because of their devotion to each other, Anna endured without complaint the long sleepless nights, observing her husband's pain with a helplessness that brought tears to her eyes. Despite many consultations with a number of doctors, and a desperate prescription of different drugs, Oscar's health continued to deteriorate until Anna saw in his face a gauntness which told her that he had reconciled himself to death.

One measure of their unquestionable devotion to each other was the fact that they had not had sex before they married, that they had both come to the wedding bed as virgins, to the best of their totally trusting knowledge of each other. Anna recalled this bond of celibacy with quiet pride when some of her women friends boasted about

4

Taï ubert

the surreptitious premarital fumbling sessions they had had with their future husbands. And even with other men. Anna was not in any way prudish though and enjoyed making love to Oscar. He, always aware of the nuances of meaning that words created, corrected her: *We make love with each other, not to each other.* And Oscar never demanded anything more than the caresses that Anna permitted. He stopped kissing her and pressing up against her body as soon as she felt his passion was becoming too fierce and asked him to stop.

There arose in her an inexplicable discomfort when Oscar's sexual desires became too intense. In the midst of their normally courteous lovemaking, a sudden wave of pure lust would surge through him. He would close his eyes as if to contain some unbearable pain within himself, his penis swelled, became huge and vividly veined like volcanic rock. But he always subsided the moment Anna whispered, *Oscar, no please.*

In the beginning of their marriage this distressed Anna, who feared that she could not satisfy Oscar's sexual needs. She remembered someone telling her that the key to a good marriage was sexual compatibility, that her father had taken a mistress because her mother was unresponsive and saw sex as no more than a duty to which all women coldly submitted. But Oscar showed great understanding and patience, sensing her struggle with the image of a placid Oscar transformed into someone fierce by his sexual desires. She loved him with great tenderness in those moments, as he kneeled on the bed before her, his head bowed, ashamed of the extraordinary appetite for sex he had displayed. He would only lie down beside her when his erection had drooped and his penis had shrunk to an appropriate, contrite size. They would caress each other to sleep, she in the crook of his arm, sheltered by his cool and gentle breathing.

Now Anna could not sleep at all. Oscar shuddered and groaned, and though the air seemed strangely sweeter and less polluted in the morning, they both rose from their bed hollow-eyed and exhausted. Anna developed an itchy skin which their latest doctor ascribed to a lack of proper sleep. The doctor, whose flabby chest reminded Anna of her mother's sad and sagging breasts in the last months of her life, was ominously named Dr Mayat, which in Arabic means "Dr Funeral". He gave Anna a limited supply of powerful sleeping pills, cautioning her against abusing them.

It could be dangerous, even fatal.

Anna sat on her side of the bed, facing away from Oscar, and swallowed, with the aid of a large glass of water, the fat and translucent capsule. She remembered Dr Mayat's immaculate fingers handling the drugs as if they were precious pearls he was counting. And how Aunt Hilda, who had left her husband and children in

6

their home by the sea to come and assist Anna, had uttered a restrained admonishment when the doctor left.

He is Indian?

Anna only turned to join Oscar in bed when she was certain he had completed his own nightly ritual, slowly drinking the many potions, capsules and tablets prescribed by specialists of all sorts.

The sleeping pills worked at first and Anna quickly sank into a state of unconsciousness the moment she shut her eyes. Her repose, however, lacked the regenerating qualities of a true and gentle slumber. Soon, even that drug-induced sleep became impossible.

Anna was compassionate and loving even though despair gnawed at the resolve she had formed in her mind *to stand by my husband*. It was discovered that the "condition", as the doctors called the illness they could not diagnose, forced Oscar to reverse his perfect breathing rhythm. He breathed in through his mouth and out through his nose. Try as he might, he could not curb this shocking deviation. He tried to compensate by breathing in and out through his mouth, which is what many men are forced to do, although not at so young an age. The snores that result from this peculiarly male malady are in themselves unpleasant. But nothing as thin and knifelike as the sounds Oscar made the moment he lay down. It was as if the very tendons of life around them were being severed. The plants which someone had advised them to bring into the room in order to increase the "natural oxygen level" seemed to stir and struggle against some unnatural presence.

Even the shafts of moonlight on the richly coloured wooden floors acquired a jaggedness that terrified Anna. She lay in bed, rigidly still, her horror impervious to the effects of the all-powerful sleeping pills, besieged by the sharp light and the grotesque rustling of innocent nasturtiums and shy ferns. Her heart finally betrayed the loving resolve of her thoughts.

In Anna's mind somewhere a voice was saying, *Listen, they're humping*—a voice that sounded like her own but had a vulgar timbre, hard and echoing, a childhood expression of disgust as parents moved about on a creaky bed in the room next door, a voice that came back to her like a recording. Other hands slid up her thighs and hot breath came close to her cheeks, not Oscar's, but someone she knew and loved, someone whose weight upon her she had forgotten. Or banished from her memory. All these years. Now she sat up and screamed. Martin, her brother, hovered above her, his face pleading and vicious at the same time. But Oscar could not help her now. He lay like a thin and decadent monarch upon a mound of pillows, struggling with the perversity of his breath. Carbon dioxide in, oxygen out.

It was Aunt Hilda who responded to Anna's scream and came bursting into her room. Aunt Hilda, with her brown hair flying behind her like that of a wild but matronly angel, who hugged the sobbing Anna and led her from the room, glancing hatefully at Oscar. He who had betrayed Anna by falling ill, by allowing this ugly and mysterious sickness to creep into his body like an evil spirit.

Anna's brother Martin, now the Director of the School of Psychology at the University, came in the morning and drove them away, his car taking off smoothly, almost without noise. The neighbours would appreciate this civilised decorum. It was a thought that Anna had, but one that she expected would be spoken by Aunt Hilda. They said things like that, Aunt Hilda and Martin and Martin's wife Helena, graceful Helena who awaited them, welcoming Anna with the warm grasp of her elegant hands. A cup of tea and then breakfast. Over the silence of clinking cups, knives scratching on good white china, Anna pondered her future. Martin tried to break the scraping silence by telling Anna, gently, that there was perhaps some psychological basis for Oscar's illness. *Kafka's curse*, he said, in between swallows of toast and honey and gulps of coffee. *At least we may be able to find an approach.* He turned his full attention to his sister, dear little Anna whom he dimly remembered protecting from bullies and lascivious men and other child-hood evils, and saw in her face the mirrored recognition of some terrible memory. Something that he too would not want to recall, but which he knew sat behind her eyes like the negatives of a photograph waiting to be developed.

Tears ran down Anna's cheeks and Helena was swiftly at her side, offering the musty comfort of her just-out-of-bed warmth. *Oh Martin! You say the most awful things, all at the wrong moment,* Helena said, before looking up and seeing Diana, her youngest daughter, standing at the foot of the stairs. Helena's embracing attention was trans-ferred to the sleepy eleven-year-old, who rubbed her eyes and pouted her pale ruby lips. Soon another daughter came thumping down the car-peted stairs. Greetings were hastily exchanged, with shy pauses when it came to Anna's turn, but the interruption was momentary and the voices soon resumed their heady flow, coffee was slurped, cheeks kissed, doors opened and shut with friendly, familial haste. Both Martin and Helena were gone from the table, miraculously clothed and briefcased, two cars left the leafy driveway with the now acceptable noise of screeching tyres. In the silence, Aunt Hilda and Anna con-templated the chaos of a leftover breakfast, the half-eaten bowls of cereal and bits of toast marooned in cups of coffee allowed to go cold because of the endless chatter. These abandoned repasts seemed to Anna to have an inherent affection, reminiscent of her own childhood. She remembered how her father had allowed his puritan attitude towards wastefulness to lapse, but only at breakfast. As if it was a ritual, the daily bending of his rigid soul. Anna remembered, as well, her mother's stern intrusion, the alien sound of her little, hasty footsteps, the glass door to the dining-room opening abruptly, and her father wiping away the crumbs of his merriment. The napkin, neatly folded into a square, would be left on the place-mat as he pushed his chair away.

Aunt Hilda wiped her mouth with the same swift gesture, rose and excused herself, a dark, brooding-hen look in her eyes that Anna remembered her aunt having had many years before she had children to brood over. Anna listened to Aunt Hilda's fingers punch the long-distance number of her home into the cordless telephone, a subtle electronic language that echoed through an extension somewhere in the house. How different all of this was. Here her brother lived, someone she vaguely loved, despite some terrifying secret slowly finding its shape in her mind's eye. Lived like a stranger with his blonde-haired wife and two children who seemed to move, when awake, with the bounding energy of aliens. Whose home was a splendour of modern angles, austere in their tall shapes, yet somehow concealing all the ostentation that her brother Martin was drawn to, not Helena, whose only flamboyance was the fluffy tiger-head slippers she wore around the house. Helena was a professor in her own right, this "own right" being more precious because it had been doubly earned.

Anna's own house seemed darker. More Oscar's house than hers, she thought, bought a long time ago with the one windfall that Oscar's freelance work as an architect had brought them. For most of his life Oscar had worked in an office and earned a comfortable enough living. The independence of his talent, which he refused to subject to the trials of a go-it-alone business, despite his brother-in-law's urging, brought huge commissions to his employer. Oscar and Anna were wealthy enough to give modestly to charity. There was nothing, really, wanting in their lives.

But Oscar, a man who refused to be stirred by the passionate debates about the political situation, the violence and the crime, the homeless people who were squatting in the suburbs and were said to be bringing the property values down, developed a stubborn protectiveness towards the house. He repaired and restored, obsessively battling the effects of the house's ninety-year-long decline, but refused to touch the structure, marvelling out loud at the *clean and simple lines*. Even the strange fountain that stood in the centre of the path leading to the front door, forcing people to confront the sorrowful sight of a castrated David, his drooping stone penis broken at the tip like a child's pee-pee. It was an *integral part of the house's nature,* Oscar said.

Anna hated the fountain's pretentiousness, but was convinced by Oscar not to have it removed, even though the jargon he used in his arguments seemed false and out of character. For the first time since she had known Oscar, she saw a desperation in his eyes. The kind of desperation, she now suspected, that he had suppressed behind his shut eyelids when overcome by his occasional, ferocious passion.

The furnishings matched the house, dignified, classic, solid. No gimmicky twists of steel or surrealistic plastic. They both had chosen that furniture, Anna because she preferred the cosy atmosphere created by the often jarring "collectedness" of the pieces bought at random, Oscar because he liked the feeling that the hands of their human creators were touching you when you sat down in them or ran the palm of your hand over a grainy wooden surface. *Affectionately, without any sexual meaning or anything like that,* he had hastily added.

But Anna saw the disdain on Martin's face on the rare occasions when her brother visited. *It's Oscar's choice, this mishmash of colours and dull shapes.* Anna read this in Martin's mind, concealed behind the unwizened brow that shaped his smile and hooded his eyes. Even Helena, magnanimous Helena could not help a wry grimace, quickly absorbed into her flashing smile. This was Oscar's house. It bore Oscar's personality, the tedious evenness of his nature. Not Anna. *She's one of us.*

What they really meant was: *Oscar's not one of us.* He was a mixture, Javanese and Dutch and Indian and God knows what else, they would later discover. He was the lovely hybrid whom Anna had fallen in love with, perhaps because of his hybridity. Only Caroline, Anna's elder sister, seemed to understand. Until Anna confided her intention to marry Oscar.

Gorgeous, all brown bread and honey! Good enough for bed . . . but to marry? That's another story, Caroline said in her wink-wink manner. *Remember Jean-Pierre? French Canadian, my eye. Good local coloured stock. A damn good fuck, though.*

In later years Caroline would marry a dentist and move to Australia.

No, she didn't really understand this love. Nor would Aunt Hilda or Martin and Helena or their children Allison and Diana. They too would marry like their parents, in search of comfort and compatibility. Somehow, in between it all, they'd try and find some passion. There would always be careers and children and concerns about the levels of violent crime to distract them from their loneliness.

Anna's father Patrick did not seem offended by Oscar's "Jewishness". *Of course, we're mixed too. Some Jewish blood in our distant pasts, but that's okay, everyone has Jewish blood in them,* Patrick said laconically. His wife Grace, the distracted mother of Caroline and Martin and Anna, frowned and fumed and finally forgave. But never approved.

A woman came into the kitchen and began to clear away the breakfast. She was dressed in a smart domestic's uniform, black with a white collar. Deft hands sorted vegetables and leaves the elder daughter had half eaten, separated their limp virtue from the more grisly remains of egg-yolks and bacon rinds. Martin's household was "green"; organic discards for their garden, washable cloth napkins instead of forest-consuming paper towels. There was a benevolent design to their extravagance, this waste of food recycled to produce more wasted food. Whereas Oscar and Anna had murdered ants and exterminated termites all their lives with ozone-depleting poisons in order to preserve a house full of gloomy artifice. Leftover food that could not be resurrected for lazy TV dinners was given to beggars in the park.

Anna remembered that Martin had named his first child "Allison-Anne" against the wishes of his wife. *It is so primitive, children should have names of their own, not some heirloom they can't discard!* She remembered too Helena's astonishing anger, the vehemence in her tired voice. Helena was right. They would hire a woman whose name

was Anne, had an aunt named Anna who would
come in sadness to live in their house.

The morning slid into a brass-sunned afternoon. The misery of the sleepless night, the early
departure past the park and its sketch-book lake,
were already forgotten. And Oscar hung like a
grey shadow of grief over Anna, like someone
already dead, transformed from loved to beloved. There arose in her consciousness the image
of a gravestone, tall marble that gleamed in the
sun. The shape of Oscar's face was slowly absorbed into its hard, detached surface.

Evening arrived quietly, doors opened with
sighs of welcoming relief, and Martin and Helena
sank back into the cool shadows of their home.
Domestic-Anne served drinks beneath the canopy
of yellowing, unharvested grapes—*Oh no, we
don't pick them, just keep them for the birds.* Their
children too joined in this ceremonial draining
away of the day's pressures, sipping soft drinks
while Martin and Helena drank chilled white
wine. That was how their relationship began,
with glasses of white wine in Helena's student
room, before they crept into her bed and muffled
their cries. Before Allison was conceived and
imposed upon them a quiet marriage in court, followed by a luncheon for friends and drunken sex
in the afternoon.

*Christ, is that what we've got now? A mere rela-
tionship?* Martin's gung-ho humour unsettled
Anna, who held her gin-and-tonic too tightly and

drank it too quickly. Aunt Hilda was doing the same, Anna suspected. Above them the rapacious rejoicing of feasting birds, and all around, the banter of sharp voices as the Martin-Helena-Allison-Diana unit used up the vestiges of their daytime adrenaline. Their decline thereafter was fast.

Not before a slightly drunken Martin resolved the problem of their names. *We'll call Anne Annie, and Anna Anna. No one calls Allison anything but Allison these days!*

Annie cleared away the dinner table, Helena prowled about for a while in tiger-patterned slippers, then went to the study, where she sat with her notes before her, absorbing the dull steep of words into her sleepy mind. Martin and young Diana fell asleep before the TV. Allison had retired long ago and and lay formally asleep in her bed, legs stretched out and arms crossed as if to ward off unwelcome dreams.

Only Aunt Hilda dutifully sat until the end with her grieving niece, observing from time to time Anna's features, drawn tight around her skull like a mask. Aunt Hilda would convey this martyrdom to her cluck-clucking husband. *She sat there like a ghost, not saying anything, so sad. Not at all like my brother who could laugh at things. Must be Grace's blood. To do all those queer things. Well, marry that crazy God-knows-what-not for starters!*

Then Aunt Hilda was gone, back to her home

by the sea, and Martin went away on conventions, and Helena with great kindness told Anna to make herself at home. *This is your home now!*

Annie cooked and cleaned and did not say much. Summer disappeared and the vine shrank into a gnarled skeleton without birds, the evening drinks were taken earlier and Martin, when he was home, sprawled on the settee until Helena led him to his bed. Anna lay in her guest-room, listening to the night noises. Martin and Helena's bed very rarely creaked and their children slept with well-fed soundness now that Allison had abandoned her leaf-and-root diet. The silence was modern, the echo of wind in symmetrical empty spaces, the hum of the refrigerator, the distant buzz of the answering machine set to low, the rapid flush of a toilet somewhere. The nearest Anna came to identifying something of the wilderness that existed beyond Martin's high, purple walls and electric gates was the lapping of water, and knew in her heart that it was the swimming-pool. Its noise was too rhythmic and ordered. In any case, they were too far from the lake.

Anna went for walks along avenues that were cold because of the looming evergreen trees. Saw old people walk their stiff-limbed dogs and did not think consciously of how youth imitated age through prolonged exposure. Anna did not regard herself as younger than them, despite their slow and carefully measured steps, even though she was about to turn only thirty-three. Nothing died here, except the vine and Anna's memory of her past life.

The occasional intrusion arrived from her house-and-life near the park. First the maid Wilhelmina, who came out of courtesy to say she was leaving, had no need to *live like that*. A new government was about to be elected, and she wanted to be home with *her* people to see one of her *own* become the country's president. And then the monthly cheques from the attorneys who had been instructed to pay Anna a pension. She showed no interest, and it was left to Martin to open an account and deposit the cheques. *You'll need it one day. No one has too much, ever.*

Anna was no recluse, and participated in the life that Martin-Helena-Allison-Diana created. She was angry enough, like Martin when Mr Mandela dared to say he would retaliate against "right-wing terror". *How dare he, what irresponsibility, isn't there enough violence?* But spoke little and smiled and cooked and helped Annie around the house. The occasional chore to keep her busy, nothing stressful. Helena saw to that.

But still Anna could not sleep and soon knew all the different cadences of sound that this soundless house made. Her ears learned to recognise the footsteps as people padded about at night, Helena's luxurious slipper-lisp, Martin's heavy stumbling stealth—a habit of old. Allison and Diana were more difficult to decipher, with their secret children's-tread, their subterfuge of weight shifting without pattern. Anna listened because she had no choice, found beauty in the ghostliness of these myriad, hidden noises because insomniacs are not spared the detail in the brush of sounds, no matter how hurried.

She did not pay any attention at first to the quiet frenzy of feet, first Martin-stumble-bumble, then Helena-lisp-and-wisp, the subdued screams, Helena sobbing, Allison murmuring and moaning, Diana standing silently in a darkened hallway. And down there, in the end, in the depths of the house that the living room became at night, Martin's silent agonies exhaled, his body rocking to and fro, disturbing the eddies of air that constituted the tranquillity of the early-hour night.

They have arguments, they are human, Anna thought out loud. Until her graven voice brought Diana into her room and into her bed. Tears from the child's face wet Anna's hair, filled her room with the wild smell of fear. And Martin outside, whispering, *Di? It's all right, it's all right!*

Anna held the child to her breasts, felt her little-girl coldness, consoled an inconsolable awareness in her staring eyes. And Helena alongside Martin, *My God, how could you? Even Di? Our little Di? And now Anna will know as well.* The shuffle of slow and humbled feet, a door shut, a scream, a sob. Diana fell asleep in Anna's arms while Anna fell asleep as if through a trapdoor in Diana's terror. And saw the quick emergence of

the ancient photograph behind her eyes, like picnic images from a one-hour processing machine.

Martin much younger, Martin monstrous,
Martin pained, Martin doubled up with agony,
Martin naked, Martin remorseful, Martin bloated
and huge, exploding in the air. Bloody confetti
fell from the sky, snowflakes thick and dark like
menstrual blood. Anna landed upon this cushion
of her womanhood remembered, and dreamed of
Oscar's house near the park. Oscar's house, filled
with his breathing presence, overflowing with
wild green foliage and flowers, fuchsias and
freesias, long-stemmed roses and roses that imposed themselves on stems gnarled like the arms
of boastful men, flowers of such variety that
Anna dreamed of exotic forests where birds cried
mournful preening cries and fell from the trees
because of the beauty of those whom they loved.
His eyes were there, Oscar's deep-set bastard
eyes, suddenly heavy-browed with leaves like
some olive-skinned beauty that Anna had seen
somewhere, his eyes and his voice were in her
sleep and its comforting refuge of dreams.

The next morning Anna walked down the
stairs to breakfast, holding a sleepy Diana by the
hand. There was an air of absence, the door ajar,
Helena's smaller German car gone. Helena and
Martin sat at the table, the food on their plates
untouched. Both seemed stiff and propped up like
shop-window dummies; Martin's air of rigid dignity gave him the appearance of beautiful fragility

this morning. Some decision had been made during the night, some agonising resolve that had emptied Helena of her dissolving warmth. A thin and sinewy being had emerged from the larva of her practised motherhood. When she spoke at last, it was quickly and coldly, her lips twitched, weariness gathered in fine lines around her eyes. Some great truth uttered had shattered her beguiling reticence.

Allison is gone. She is old enough, heaven knows, to take care of herself, Helena said and took a sip of coffee. She glanced up at Martin, who blinked and forced his eyes to swallow the fat tears swimming at their edges. *Anna, please take care of Di for a while. You should stay here. But if you want, take Di to Oscar's house. We're going away for a while, Martin and I.*

Between gulps of coffee that Annie brought her, Anna told the uncomprehending Helena and Martin of her dream during the night. Not her dream of Martin, or even of Oscar, but of a story that Oscar had told her once, when his tongue and his imagination had momentarily been freed from their architect's stricture.

You see, Anna said, *he remembered his beginnings when he had a bit of wine. And told me the story of Leila and Majnoen. Now Majnoen is both a name and a madness . . . In Arabia, I think—where else would he set his beginnings?—there lived a beautiful princess named Leila whom everybody wanted to marry. That's what people want from princesses. Marriage . . .*

But she fell in love with her father's gardener Majnoen, a gifted man, but strange. He talked to trees and whispered to flowers and could make things grow just by breathing on them. Of course, no princess could freely marry a gardener, so they agreed to run away. They were to meet in the forest which Majnoen knew like no one else, every tree, leaf and grassy path. Majnoen promised his beloved that he would wait for her, no matter what. But the inevitable happened . . . Leila's father the caliph found out about their intention to run away and because he could not live with the shame of his daughter going off with a common gardener, a mud-fingers, he locked her up. And Majnoen waited, for days, for weeks, until the seasons changed, until the forest worried about him, his hunger and his thirst; and began to feed him. Sunshine and rain, and rich black earth, protected him from worms and woodborers and so forth. When at last Leila managed to escape and hurried to where she was to meet Majnoen, she found that he had become part of a tree . . . no . . . he had become a tree! Not an ugly old oak, but a beautiful and sensitive willow.

Finally Anna wiped her mouth and took Diana upstairs to wash and dress. Helena had only a momentary pang of regret, a vague worry about this crazy old aunt's ability to look after her daughter. But remembered that Anna was not

23

that old, and that she had regained her smile. And she had a sense of humour.

How wise not to speak of our pain, Martin's pain in particular.

By the time Anna had packed and come downstairs, Helena and Martin were gone. She called a taxi and asked Annie to lock up the house.

And oh, your name is Anne, not Annie, Anna said to the bemused woman, who locked the door and watched the taxi leave the driveway, strangely unworried about her future.

They run away all the time, these people, she said to herself.

You're sure this is the right place? the taxi-driver asked Anna as he pulled up at the address she had given him.

Yes, she answered brusquely, though she too felt a little uncertain.

She paid the driver and waved him off as soon as he had removed their suitcases from the back of the car. His apprehension only added to her own. She stood on the pavement like someone who had returned after a long absence to surroundings she no longer recognised. Trees that she remembered as innocuous shrubs had changed their character, grown tall and intertwined their branches to hide the house from view. Even the wisteria creeper, an unimaginative plant which bloomed briefly, and dutifully, each spring, seemed to have clambered up pillars and guttering and colonised the roof. Most mysterious of all was the foliage draped around David's torso like some emperor's cloak. The statue's stone face had not lost its arrogant expression. At least that was familiar, as was the dry fountain and the magnolia tree.

Although it had appeared derelict at first glance, the garden was well tended. The grass had been cut recently and the path was free of invading weeds, the first signs of an abandoned property.

Diana clung to the gate, peering through the ornate metalwork. *Come on, Auntie, we have to go in,* she said in an insistent, almost Martin-like voice.

It was then that Anna saw Wilhelmina, their former domestic worker, seated in the magnolia's wide shade. Wilhelmina spoke to a man who lay on the grass, and he raised himself onto his elbows to look at Anna and Diana. His bare chest made Anna uncomfortable. Wilhelmina spoke quietly again, and the man rose, slowly put on his shirt, and walked towards the back of the house. Now Wilhelmina stood up and looked directly at Anna.

Anna stopped herself from calling out a delighted greeting.

So good to see a familiar face.

Wilhelmina's eyes were hard.

So, you're back, Anna imagined the woman saying, and silently began rehearsing her own response. A mixture of remorse—*It was not easy for me to leave*—and anger—*Why do I have to justify myself to you?*

This is still my house, Anna ended up saying in her mind.

Do you have a key, Auntie? Diana called out.

Yes, I have a key.

To Anna's relief, the key fitted the lock perfectly. The heavy gate swung back on rusty hinges. She dragged their suitcases into the garden and locked the gate behind her. Then she turned to Wilhelmina, determined to overcome the feeling that she, Anna, was an intruder.

A polite exchange took place between them.

When did you come back?

After the elections.

You've taken care of the place very nicely. Thank you.

They paused.

Wilhelmina and her husband Isaiah, the man Anna had just seen, had found the place deserted when they returned. The garden was wild, like the bushveld, overgrown with grass and thorn-trees and weeds. They cleaned it up. They painted the back rooms, fixed the leaking taps and unblocked the drains. Rats had nested in the car abandoned in the garage, and so they put out poison.

They lived at the back and never used the front gate. They had never gone into the house or tried to open it—even though Wilhelmina had a key.

Now Wilhelmina offered that key to Anna. Anna smiled and revealed her own set of keys in the palm of her hand. Another shadow of antagonism passed between them.

Oh, I work in the city, Wilhelmina said. She would pay *something*. She would not reassume the role of servant, nor would she move out. She and Isaiah had done too much to rescue the back quarters from inevitable ruin. This was silently understood.

Anna mentally readied herself to enter the house. It seemed enclosed, like a crypt. It's those shutters which Oscar refused to remove. They belong to cold places, places not used to the sun. She would have them taken down immediately.

What awaited her inside? When she'd informed the police of her intention to return, they had warned her to expect the worst. *After all, your husband lay dead there for many months before the neighbours called us. We traced his relatives, but they said there wasn't much left of the body to bury. It was as if it had crumbled to dust.*

Anna unlocked the door and pushed it open. Holding Diana's hand she stepped into the gloom. Wilhelmina followed, curious to know what the house looked like after being closed up for so long.

The furniture was covered with a thick layer of dust that stirred and hung in the air when Anna touched the back of a chair or ran her fingers across the long wooden table in the dining-room. In what had once been the main bedroom, a tree had thrust up through the floor. Flowers sprouted in a profusion of colours from the dark, disinterred earth, green moss covered the walls.

The air had a sweet, damp smell, like the air in a forest.

It's not as bad as it looks, Anna said.

Hayi suka! You people are absolutely mad. It is time Mandela took over the country, Wilhelmina said.

Majnoen

"MAJNOEN IS BOTH a name and a madness." Yes, Anna remembered that story I told her about the tragic lovers, Leila and Majnoen. A fairy tale, of course, embellished and embroidered and impregnated with meaning until it became a myth. All such tales lie a little, without any malicious intent. It is noble I suppose to use the gift of storytelling, that peculiar power only humans have, as far as I know, to create a whole way of life from a strand of fact, a mundane incident quickly observed. Complete with the kind of guiding philosophies and dogmas that martyrs will die for, and in defiance of which heretics are put to death. No, I am not a storyteller, a maker of myths, a spinner of yarns, whatever you want to call it. My craft is blunt and simple, and much more honest. There isn't much art in straight lines. They end up as buildings, houses, bridges, edifices that do no more than make functional other people's dreams and fantasies. We make real their follies, not our own. That's where the integrity of my profession lies: we have no pretension to art or artifice.

Perhaps that was the problem. Because I did not know much about the artistry involved in telling tales, I allowed the myth of Leila and Majnoen to lie a little more than necessary, allowed great liberties to be taken with the realities of time and place. Imagine a man turning into a tree as he waits for a lover who will never arrive. A well-deserved fate, if you ask me, for a lowly gardener waiting for a princess. In any case, there are no great forests in all of Arabia. So, what are the real origins of the legend? A trivial incident, sentimentalised and exaggerated to heroic proportions by slaves from India or Java or Malaysia to sustain themselves? A coping mechanism— that's what you call it, no? It might have been African? This continent is fecund—yes, fecund—with the kind of foliage which gives birth to the secret lives that are the very substance of magical parable. We spring our heroes on you when you least expect it, conjure them up from dusty townships, make them walk across shark-infested waters, bring them old and wizened to your doorstep in order to defeat you with their wisdom. But making it African would somehow have missed the whole point of the deception, unintended as it was.

You see, the myth really warns against the madness of Majnoen, or is it against majnoen the Madness? An insanity that strikes those who dare to stray from their "life's station", that little room which you are told at birth is yours. You may expand it a bit, add a loft or a garden, build a bigger fence than the one you inherited. But you leave it at your peril. In fact, you are punished for leaving. Look, could Majnoen help it that his father was a simple gardener, like his father before him, and so forth? Could Leila change the fact that her father was a rich and powerful caliph, who became rich and powerful because his family controlled the spice trade or bought and sold slaves? Making this tale African would have been too obvious. Everybody wants to make our little room theirs, make their destiny ours. It was Muslim, that much I know. Whoever passed it on to me must have made a very firm point of that.

Anna remembered it, because it seemed to her to be my story. Very early on, long before my brother came to our house and revealed who and what I was, I saw that she nurtured within her some cancerous intuition that I would one day be made to pay for all the straying-from-the-path I have done. That uncanny women's instinct. It enabled her to divine that, for some mysterious reason, the natural order of my being would change. Not this specific condition, this slow poisoning of my lungs caused by breathing in carbon dioxide and breathing out oxygen, blood cells carrying the toxin to the forests of my heart and the roots of my nervous system. Do you know, I can feel my brain absorb the hissing gas—this is conjecture now, a desperate envisioning of the unknown—and turn this much too exalted temple, the "home" of my soul, into a seething and sulphurous swamp.

I cannot claim that Anna brought this upon me, that for the love of her I broke the bonds of my beginnings and defied the ancient injunction not to desert the pride or clan, not to leave the village of rickety houses or climb out of the womb of our nation. Her warnings to me were as subtle and uncertain as they come, filled with the anxiety of love and the fear of loss. The fact is that I met Anna long after I had changed my name from Omar to Oscar and, by reordering one letter of the alphabet, had changed the name of my father from Khan to Kahn. The ease, the casual sleight of hand with which you could change an entire history seems lost on those who are punishing me now. If it is a "they" or a "those" and not some immutable law that I defied.

In those days—the old South Africa, you remember? Of course, you were much too young. Reality, then, was exactly what you saw. Nothing more than "face value". I was fair, and why not, my grandmother was Dutch. This oppressive country had next-to-Nazis in government, yet had a place, a begrudged place but a place nevertheless, for Jews. Can you believe it? For that eternally persecuted race?

Because they were white.

Yes, I took advantage of my fair skin. Like those Jews with blond hair and straight noses who discarded their Jewishness because it was wartime and they were being persecuted. It was a matter of life or death. Of course there are comparisons to be made. Not being able to study, to go to university, became an architect, being forced to remain Omar Khan, the son of a newly impoverished township entrepreneur, was a form of death! I changed from Omar Khan to Oscar Kahn, fair-skinned and curly-haired. A beautifully hooked nose—Anna used to suck at it, after the appropriate blowing and cleaning enabled me to cross an invisible divide. It was like leaving one dimension of the world for another, where time and place remained the same, but their surfaces had different textures. The morning noises, a frenzy of birds and hurrying footsteps, seemed purposeful and even innocent, the midday sun stopped burning your feet right through the soles of your shoes. And the nights most of all. I no longer thought of nightfall as a time when murderous eyes furtively emerged from their daytime hiding-places. Wherever those were. Funny how in the townships you never knew who was innocent and who wasn't, which bland smile during the day would turn into the murderer's smirk at night.

Omar-turned-Oscar left the townships and moved to the suburbs, where the rustle of the wind in the trees filled him with a strange peace. A little desolate and lonely, but peace nevertheless. He was overcome by a drowsiness that allowed no restlessness, that dulled the body's unexplained anxieties and demanded no sharp glance into the shadows. Noises were noises, they required no explanation and disappeared into silence. That was the marvel of this new world: how ordinary everything became. Trees creaked and gates scraped into unoiled hinges, neither necessarily signifying any kind of intrusion. In the township such noises made you tense and alert. Like a frightened animal.

Why, yes, I am talking about myself. Perhaps at that moment I was somewhere in between Omar and Oscar, in substance neither one being nor the other. But I adapted very quickly. By the time I entered the service of Meyer Lewis as a newly qualified architect, I had become completely acclimatised. I knew what the simple, white-painted sign on the front of a bus meant, boarded with absolute confidence, and was eventually able to sit and read my paper without sparing a glance at the rows of black people whom we left behind at each stop. There was a skill to this deception. The secret lay in it not being a deception at all. Omar had to become Oscar, and believe that he was Oscar.

Also, out of my patient desire to learn, I endured the way Meyer Lewis humiliated me, every day, at every opportunity, in the beginning. Captain Schmuck, he called me, after the first house I designed had the servitude on the wrong side.

"You want shit to flow where people eat? Not in Meyer Lewis's business!"

Not once did I allow that familiar feeling of grating anger, as sharp as the ribs of a township dog, to slip through the gates of my imprisoned sanity. In my dreams I often slit Meyer's bulbous throat and danced with naked feet in the pools of his hot blood. In reality I bit my volatile tongue— a curse, I think, passed down from my mother's side—even though Meyer constantly goaded me, not only finding fault but doing so with glee, publicly exposing my architectural sins in the most colourful language you can imagine. I began to hate *his* hybrid South African Yiddisher tongue, his sharp and contemptuous eyes. But there was a benevolence in his scornful tutoring, a generosity even. Perfection is not inborn, but fashioned in you. A sharp chisel and a tutor's hammer.

The beauty of it all, the perverse wonder, was that I achieved my great crossing-over with the collusion and help of my father. He was a man of little sentiment, almost Semitic in his sense of reality. You could expect no less of him, of course, if you knew a little of his own life. I wonder now what his punishment was?

I have this sudden recollection of him.

Why? I don't know. No, I don't think that Meyer became a surrogate father to me.

I remember my father Sal, short for Salaam— often mispronounced "Sally", the girl's name. He was not at all like Meyer who was short and stocky. Sal was slim. An olive-skinned swarthiness, darker than me, his hair even darker, wavy and neatly parted on the side, handsome like some half-caste god.

We went on a picnic once and ran up against a group of whites who had just been told that the earth was theirs, any part of it, all of it. My mother stood anxiously at his side.

"Please Salaam, let's go." She refused to call him by his diminutive. That was her way.

Sal leaned against the wood-panelled Cadillac he used when my mother's family joined us for Sunday outings. That's right, he had another car, a two-seater Chev with a soft top, but the Cadillac demonstrated that he was a man of substance. Part of a psychology of survival at that time. The sun cooled on his unruffled blue shirt. He walked towards a group of white men who stood at the entrance to the picnic spot, yes a public place, barring any blacks—non-whites—from going in. A lot of others had stopped, looked at the situation, and driven on. The guard was a black guy from the townships. Of course he was scared,

who wouldn't be? Beyond them, a smooth river,
a few white kids playing on its banks. The
moment was fraught with violence. Sal walked
towards the silent men, his hands thrust into the
pockets of his white trousers, testing the mettle of
their belligerence. He spoke to them in this
immaculately gruff Afrikaans you can only learn
at the feet of a mother or a grandmother. Or from
a white, Boere missus. One of thirteen languages
he could speak. Anyway, it seemed to work, to
soften the brutality of their postures. Though no
one smiled and no one moved out of the way, we
knew that a deal had been struck. Sal had that
look on his face.

"Just a bunch of poor kids from the orphanage.
Scared of dark people."

He glanced at the faces in his own entourage,
mostly my mother's family, their faces dark with
silent apprehension. "Shit, what a murderous
bunch we must seem to them!"

Beyond the unbarred gates, on the edges of the
cool water, we gambolled, our skins glowing
with well-fed health, the vigour that comes from
constant scrubbing and the softening balm of
petroleum jelly. The other kids, "poor whites"
our Aunt Hajera had called them, stopped playing, the spectacle of our joy too much to bear, the
quick darkness of our bodies in the clear water—
in the townships you learn to swim, to "goef",
very early on. And the array of fruit and meat and
bread spread out, fastidious rather than festive,

on a cloth beneath the trees. The orphans and their minders watched us, arms folded, holding back their rage. I recall their silent faces, their dead eyes. Some manly honour was at stake. They did not want to renege on a deal.

"It won't last. They'll soon realise how much power they have."

Salaam, Sal, and even Salvatore when it suited him, sat upon a tartan blanket, clutching his knees, his rueful wealth gleaming in the silk of his socks, as sleek as a woman's ankles. His wife, our mother Salma . . . yes our father's name was Salaam, our mother's Salma, a marriage designed to confuse . . . Salma, always ill at ease in the shadow of our father's sense of power, fussed over us. Our squeals of spoilt delight as our father intervened and allowed us, in the heat, the pleasure of ice-cream in place of the wholesome fare our mother, a child herself, insisted on offering. We must have planted some murderous seeds in the mind of at least one of the orphan boys. I remember, vaguely, a pair of eyes heavily browed like a peaked cap, the look of pain as a young boy turned and ran off to join the other departing orphans.

Our pleasure was spoilt as well.

"Did you give them money?" Uncle Hashim asked Sal.

My father did not answer. He stripped down to the swimming-trunks he wore beneath his trousers and walked towards the river. Uncle Hashim pursued him, stopping only when the mud became too thick. Sal, of course, stood there, allowing the sludge to squelch pleasurably between his toes.

"How much did you give them, this Helpmekaar Home?"

Uncle Hashim was screaming by now. My father dived into the water. I knew how cold it was, it took our breath away when we first went in. Yet he just swam into the middle, without so much as a shiver, and drifted about in the calm current where the water was deepest. I looked at the faces of the adults around me.

Uncle Hashim's was purple. That's the colour dark people go when they get really angry. He was my mother's eldest brother, the head of the family since the death of his father. He had performed the customary "giving away" ceremony at her wedding. Now this arrogant man whom he, Hashim, had allowed his sister Salma to marry, ignored his authority. Treated him with open disrespect.

He turned to my mother, whose face, like that of her mother and her sister Hajera, had turned a sick colour, drained of life. Three outlandishly dressed porcelain figurines—yes, they went picnicking in ribbons and bows—glazed over with fear and embarrassment. Hashim had been promising this "to-do" with Salaam for a long time.

"He has no respect, this husband of yours. All I wanted to know was how much he gave them.

He lacks the decency, the upbringing to answer me."

Finally Ouma Kulsum, Sal's mother and our grandmother, answered Uncle Hashim. "What's it got to do with you? It's his money."

Her face, when Sal dived into the water, had frozen, as if she was reliving a terrifying experience. Her real name was Katryn. The daughter of a poor Afrikaner smallholder, she had taken the name Kulsum for the man she loved, Shaik, Sal's father. Shaik had shot himself many years ago for no other reason than to see what death was like. I would discover later on that my father was not a good swimmer. When he dived into the deceptively slow-flowing river, he had risked his life. Maybe to see what drowning was like.

"Black-market money!"

"He bought what was available and sold to those who wanted it. Business. Nothing else."

"A bribe. He paid a bribe for this . . . this stinking bit of pleasure."

"Helpmekaar is—"

"A home for whites only, for blerry Boere children only. You see anything but damn Boere among them?"

"So that's it? Colour?"

"You blerry right, that's it. Damn colour."

My first observation of the war of the worlds. Uncle Hashim growing hoarse, waving his arms, stamping his feet to get the mud off his shoes and to ease the strain on his heart, blerrying and damning in a way that shocked all of us. What had really hurt him, caused his rather melodramatic outburst, still escapes me. Ouma Kulsum, in her aloof whispering voice, hid another kind of pain. Something that went beyond just being called a "blerry Boer".

My father emerged from the water breathing a bit heavily. He caught Ouma Kulsum's eye and shook his head, urging her not to argue against Uncle Hashim's dull righteousness. He dried himself, watching my mother all the time, the catatonic expression on her face.

"The problem with us non-whites is we have no pride," Uncle Hashim muttered through his morose beard. His opposition to what my father had done—so simple an act of accommodation—was unrelenting.

"Let him walk home," Ouma Kulsum said as we climbed into the car.

Sal smiled, he always did that when there was nothing to be done, when something was about to happen and there was no stopping it. Our mother clambered into the back with her mother, her sister and brother—four aggrieved adults in the back of a station-wagon!—their solidarity as uncomfortable as any squashed-together human patriotism. We knew that when we reached home Sal would leave, walk out into the township darkness, while we played awkwardly in the gloomy world of disaffected adults, my brother Malik and I.

Our spinsterish aunt Hajera and our "other" grandmother whose name we never really knew would leave full of remorse that they had somehow been the cause of conflict in Salma's home. Uncle Hashim remained unrepentant. "It is better to know what this man is, know it now," he warned his sister.

Malik and I sat up with my mother. She had this look of love on her face that made both of us want to crawl into her arms. But the moment we moved closer to her, she became distant, as if she was afraid of what this intimacy would bring. More loss, or the fear of loss. Eventually we fell asleep on the settee. She maintained her upright vigil, sitting next to us, her hands folded in her lap.

She was beautiful. Straight out of a Gauguin canvas. Dark and thin with long black hair. No, the description is not too exotic. Take a walk around the streets of Cape Town, you'll see women like her everywhere.

Why did she wait up for my father?

I think because she knew that one night he would not come back. Run over by a car, mugged in some dark street, assassinated by a business rival, killed by a jealous husband, who knows? My father lived a predestined life, or so he said. Yes, perhaps it was an excuse for not taking any moral responsibility for his actions. He always did what was *necessary*.

Simple, choose between what is necessary and what is not.

Anyway, she waited alone for my father to return. And that night he did come home, smelling of smoke and whisky, a dull contentment in him brought about by the many wagered hands of poker he'd played with other men as smoothly shaven and perfumed as he. We heard them speak in their bedroom. Even our township palace had its limitations. Rooms too small and walls too thin.

"Don't let this bullshit about being right or wrong destroy our children. Listen, out there an animal is prowling around. It's looking for people like you and your family to eat. Because you're weak and you're slow. Don't teach my sons to be weak and slow."

Well, he said something like that. And she? She protested, mildly, about the need to teach children some morality.

My father was right about the Afrikaners realising the extent of their power. They would use it first to become rich. Ideology and morality would follow. The ethical among them would protest mildly. They clawed back the wealth my father had earned by selling white sugar and flour to poor white families during the war, wealth for which he had risked death as a black marketeer, until he owned shops and homes that they declared "white" and expropriated. They went further, said that my grandfather had never paid taxes, that he had been a profiteer who exploited poor whites and blacks alike. Now the new morality was being defined. The good white man would wreak justice in the name of the simple black man. Of course, you can guess. There were people, suddenly in power, who could not forgive my grandfather his white wife, their aunt, their mother's sister, the living shame of a white hoer and her hoer child.

So the State taxed and expropriated. Sal fought back. Until his ingenuity was exhausted or those whom he bribed acquired a greed beyond his reach, until they found other, worthier fools to blackmail and intimidate.

"Go," he said, "here's the last of it. Don't be poor and proud."

My brother walked away, chewing his tongue as was his nervous habit, full of scorn and anger. He refused this gift of thief's gold. Oh yes, we knew all about our father's criminality, about him being a black marketeer. It was all in the papers. My father stepped off a pavement one day, into the path of a speeding ambulance.

"Trust him," they said.

To be more dramatic than the dying and the damned. I didn't make it to his funeral, to observe the many tears of bitter hypocrisy that Sal had prophesied, because Meyer Lewis offered me an opportunity that would never come again, the chance to design and build a huge tower with a revolving restaurant at the top. In Durban, near Grey Street. Alongside Muslim minarets and Hindu temples and Holy Roman cathedrals would rise this phallus. Apartheid with its balls up.

I'm sorry.

"Have no illusions about their taste," Meyer said, "it stinks. But they're paying."

He smiled at me with genuine affection for the first time. I went to Durban and didn't think my father would mind. I knew that one day I would face my mother's sadness and my brother's abhorrence. That's life.

It was sweet Anna who met me at the station and guided me by taxi to the squat row of houses where The Tower was to be built. People came onto their verandas to stare at yet another grey-suited man surveying the impending ruination of their lives.

"Shit, he looks like a Chaar, just like us!" one of them said.

"Are you Indian?" Anna asked once we were back in the taxi.

The innocence in her face made me hesitate, but I recovered quickly enough to lie without a blush. "No, the Kahn here is a good old Jewish name," I said, avoiding the eyes of the sneering taxi-driver.

I stayed behind in Durban and designed The Tower with the revolving restaurant where people could dine and stare out over the oily har-

bour and the sluggish sea beyond. The gentle
motion caused a slight sensation of disorientation
and increased the desire to drink, it was said. A
slow vertigo of the senses, what a wonderful way
to die. They stopped the place from turning on its
own axis after three diners had thrown themselves into the street below. Like lemmings they
leapt through the same window in a reception
area designed to capture the merging of light
from the sea and the city. During its construction
I'd had a forboding about this room, with its walls
of glass that gave it the appearance of a derelict
spaceship. I made sure that the mechanism on
which it would turn was solid and without fault.

I courted Anna and learned not to react to the
stares of people, black and white and Indian. We
were a young couple, full of laughter and life.
The first time I persuaded her to go to bed with
me, in the little flat within sight of The Tower's as
yet skeletal construction, she refused to have sex,
but allowed me to kiss her all over, and then
watched me masturbate. She was not surprised
that I was circumcised; a Jewish custom after all.
I remember her wondering at the smoothness of
my penis. It was the cry of joy I uttered when I
reached my climax that seemed to surprise or
even shock her.

No, it's not the same as having sex. Her not
being penetrated was the chasteness. I don't think
that's a mere male fantasy.

The point is that I had to learn to mute my cry of love, reduce it to a low and incomprehensible moan. Even I did not understand the language that flowed from me when at times I was caught in the vortex of sexual pleasure. After we were married. We had sex—penetration—for the first time on our wedding night. There were times when I was overcome by an uncontrollable, tongue-babbling desire for sex. Against my will and my better intentions I must add. I was driven to betray Anna, who was too gentle to understand this need to find an outlet for the voice of my passion. The occasional prostitute, the cleanest on offer, I made certain of this, and usually warned her beforehand of my single perversion—"No, no, nothing of that sort, just a desire to scream, can be quite deafening," I had to reassure many a nervous young woman.

But we were happy in the main, Anna and I. We were married according to Christian rites, at Anna's request. To please her family, even though only her brother attended the wedding. It was Meyer's good word that brought her father onto our side and prevented her mother—from a good old Natal family, very British—from seeking all sorts of court injunctions.

Anna's mother hated me. I think she suspected even my Jewishness. Prejudice has unerring instincts. I knew that my papers would stand up to legal scrutiny, for my father had known how to get to the right people. It was probably some manner or mannerism, a mispronounced word, a plural verb in the wrong place, some inherent fault-line in the crust of my being, that confirmed her suspicions. "I am not an Asquill for nothing," she once said, as if her sugar-baron family name was a divining device as well as an intimidating title. But she said nothing, not then anyway. I think old Patrick Wallace was looking for an excuse to murder her. Humiliate his darling daughter? He would not allow that to happen. In any case, as soon as we could, Anna and I moved to Johannesburg. People in Natal it seemed had it in their genes to smell out bastard Asian blood.

With the proceeds of The Tower commission—Meyer now displayed an extraordinary generosity, just loved my "chutzpah", he said— we bought this old house near the park, this house of gnarled character, floors of wood polished to a gleaming smoothness like ageing skin, mottled veins in its grain and knots of history which recorded the bruised passage of naked feet, the scuffing of claw-footed tables and chairs upon which posteriors ponderously sat or mischievously shifted, where knees and thighs were explored by adventurous hands. The house had an air of audacious illicitness. Cosy window-seats, ornate ceilings in which you could see on insomniac nights the pressed images of forbidden lusts, the indelicate beauty of curved shapes and arched flowers. To this house of concealed smells and surreptitious shadows we brought our rather commonplace love.

We slowly imposed our modest tastes upon the house. Settees, paintings, asymmetrical chairs. The haphazard way in which we bought furniture brought a derisive smile to Martin's face. Our things didn't suit the house's design, and I sometimes imagined that the sound of the wind in its old-fashioned eaves was a lament. Unlike Martin, though, who expressed his opinions with a lisping slyness, the house cried its discontent out loud. We were too conventional, I think, to satisfy its garish instincts or perpetuate the subtle, aberrant history which I now suspect we inherited.

Yes, I disliked Martin. There was something brittle in him. An evil that perhaps even he wasn't conscious of. He very rarely visited us. But always on an occasion when something happened to disturb the tranquillity of our lives. He was there with his wife Helena and their two children when my brother arrived. I recognised Malik even before his car stopped and he had alighted. A white djellaba flowed over his suddenly ample paunch, a soft embroidered kofiya covered his head. A caricature of himself, a real Malik-ul-Mout, Angel of Death, conveying with his dark and sad eyes the news of someone's passing. And I knew that it was our mother even before he uttered the words, "Mother is dead."

All the scorn he had borne towards me and

towards "these people" who were now my family was concentrated in Malik's bearing. A township slouch, the weight of his body supported on one leg, a bird of prey and a bird preyed upon, always ready to take flight. His hands behind his back held the keys to his car and house and whatever else he owned, jangled in the still air, a metallic music of defiance. But the duel was between him and Martin, we all saw the slashes of light clash like swords between their silhouettes.

My second observation of the war of the worlds.

No, the antagonism was not between good and evil or between black and white. I'm still not sure why they became the poles between which I had to choose. I chose neither, of course, and that is when all this began.

I remember Anna at my side, walking with me to the gate. I had changed into dark, sombre clothes and heavy shoes. I felt the constricting heat of Omar's hands around Oscar's throat in the collar of my shirt, which I had buttoned up tightly, but out of embarrassment resisted Anna's attempts to loosen it, to give me air.

What a hold the woman has on him, Malik would think.

Suddenly I felt overcome by the clumsy fierceness Uncle Hashim used to display whenever women fussed over him, his mother, my mother, the girl whom he courted and who seemed too young, too alive for him. "Figure Baby", my

mother called Warildia, and warned her brother
about girls who wore their belts so tight at the
waist. I wondered what had become of Uncle
Hashim. Did he marry Warildia Figure Baby,
how many children did they have and where did
they live? What little tragedy had my uncle set in
motion?

"Would you like me to come along?" Anna
asked.

"No," I answered sternly, the image of Malik
and Martin at the fountain in the middle of the
garden like dust in my eye. The crunching sound
of Malik's footsteps. I looked back expecting to
see the awkward, stumbling brother I remembered, heavy-set, his tongue nervously stuck into
the recess of an absent tooth. But this Malik was
secure and certain in the way he walked, and his
eyes had a quiet iridescence. Martin stood at the
fountain, working with his shoe at a patch of
loose plaster. His elegant voice sounded vexed.

"You should remove this grotesque thing," he
said to Anna.

"What thing?" Anna asked distractedly. She
was observing Helena's face and their children's
averted eyes. Anna's husband, Uncle Oscar, was
no longer merely quaint or eccentric. He was
different. Not one of us.

We drove in silence, Malik taking the freeway
because he was uncertain of the quicker routes
through the northern suburbs. The emergence
from one world into the other was abrupt. I had

expected some kind of leafy farewell, the bowing of trees, the hissing of wind. We stopped quite suddenly outside my father's house, which was now Malik's. I saw that the house had been expanded to the very edge of the property, so that the constraint of space seemed more marked. Much older than the "township scheme" houses which surrounded it, Malik's Mansion, as local people now called it, retained its gracious air, but the dignity of its straight and solid form had been wounded by many grafted-on renovations.

Once inside, I was surprised by how little the house had changed, how the core of bedrooms, dining-room and lounge had resisted attempts to violate its shape. All the additions, the ugly little alcoves and arched doorways which linked one gloomy, alabaster-painted room to the other, had been attached externally. It struck me that our history is contained in the homes we live in, that we are shaped by the ability of these simple structures to resist being defiled. There, in the heart of Salaam's house—embroidered and brocaded with innocent intent but resembling a celibate whore-house—the scene had been set for the inevitable drama of our lives. Oh how we love funerals, the sad-sweet sweet-sad climax of a life given sudden significance at the very end, no matter how dull or without consequence that life has been. Here would gather children and grand-children, brothers and sisters, enemies and

friends, and even those who did not remember
my mother in such grandly intimate terms.

Hajji Salma.

Was she a Hajji?

With a family like hers, she'd better be.

But her husband?

Nog worse, her son Omar . . .

She lay on a sheet on the floor of the living
room. The ornate frames of paintings and portraits, their faces turned to the wall, revealed their
stained brown-paper backings like soiled underwear. Incense curled from tall brass holders—
bought at Moolla's in the Oriental Plaza, I
thought—a thick aroma stuck in your throat and
permeated your hair so that you smelled of death
for days. A group of women sat in vigil, their
backs against the wall, the younger ones swaying
gently to and fro. They read different passages
from the Koran, as others had done throughout the night, muttering prayers, ordering and
marshalling, like faithful servants, Koranic injunctions to mercy, to accompany my mother to
the cemetery. There, as the congregation turned
away from her grave, her innocence, my mother
Salma's almost ingenuous lack of sin and sinfulness would be tested by the wily Gabriel, arch-
angel, arch-thief, stealer of souls, angel of death.

My heart broke. Silent Salma. All the brutal
men in her life.

We buried her quickly and simply. Many hands

wrung mine in sympathy, men kissed my cheeks until the slobber began to resemble tears. God forgave the dead, we forgave each other. Malik stood beside me, serene in the authenticity of his grief. I ate food in his house, squatting on the floor like everyone else, and washed my hands with the same grave ceremony. It was Malik who said it was time to go. No one dared protest—though I saw a mild remonstrance in his wife's eyes—as he waited for me to rise so that he could drive me back to my banishment.

Anna was waiting for me, and hugged me unexpectedly as I entered. We paused in our embrace, listening to the sound of Malik driving off. The squeal of his tyres sounded angry in the quiet suburban night. It was as if he had been waiting to see whether I would be welcomed back into the arms of my deceitful life, and whether I would accept that embrace. Somehow, I think I failed, in Malik's eyes, an ultimate test.

Indeed, our time is up.

Is it helping? Yes, I expect it is.

But wait, there is one more thing I have to tell you.

That night Anna, more tender than ever before, asked me to make love to her, a very bold gesture on her part. Afterwards she lay in my arms, bathing in my sweat. Still, a night that began so sweetly became a horror of tumbling hours. Long after Anna had turned away and fallen asleep, I was besieged by voices, cajoling voices, screaming, tormenting, vilifying, voices of unspeakable grief, maddening, beautiful. It took all my will-power, and the slender anchor of Anna's curved back, to keep me from rushing out into the darkness in search of their source, gurgling like a throat that had been cut. When finally I awoke from the exhausted sleep I must have fallen into, I remembered most of all my mother's anguished voice urging me to pray, "Bacha, for a good life, bacha!" I felt Anna's fingers touch a barklike patch of skin on my back. Neither of us said anything, until it was time to rise and she whispered that she loved me, and in the turmoil of our emotions did not notice the stiffness of my limbs.

That night it began, all of this.

I WANT TO tell you about the fountain. I resolved on the night of my mother's burial that no one would remove the fountain.

Why did it become such an issue?

Anna asked the same question. She said it was not an issue . . . she did not want the fountain removed . . . I don't know. Perhaps the fountain became the symbol of my resistance—the ramparts of my soul which I thought Martin would try to breach.

Why? What did Martin want?

Anna. Anna was the prize. No, not physically. I think he accomplished that a long time ago. He wanted more than her forgiveness, he wanted her connivance, her active participation in the conspiracy that led to her violation, a conspirator herself. Sin without sinfulness, absolution without penance.

No, I'm not certain. She never talked about her childhood. It was something I guessed, the total lack of acknowledgement of Martin in her eyes, as if she recognised him externally, but did not register him in her brain, as if he was someone who did not belong in her memory.

All right, the fountain. Let's go back.

It was a simple structure. A young, boyish David had water piped up through his foot and out through his penis. The piping was made of metal and it rusted. Over time the rust coloured the water until he appeared to be peeing blood.

Yes, before we moved there, I know because I asked the neighbours. They said it was a neighbourhood curiosity. Something that Simon, the boy who lived here, was mercilessly teased about at school. Probably the school down the road. Still there today. The house is not on any particular route to buses or shops. Schoolboys in those days, it seems, deliberately walked past Simon's house to have a look at this freakish thing, a little pissing David.

In a fit of shame and anger Simon took a garden spade and lopped David's penis off. David was left with a set of stone testicles and a gaping hole through which the bloody pee now gushed.

The effete little spray was gone. David became sinister and vengeful in his grief. Simon was conscience-stricken. And humiliated. To save his son's sanity, Simon's father turned off the water and eventually removed the pump. Only some tragic death in the family, Simon's grandfather I think, saved David from complete dismemberment, stone by crumbling stone. The family left in a hurry.

I found the pump in an old shed, repaired it and replaced it, threaded plastic tubing through the existing piping. Though I could do nothing at all about David's disfigured sex. Ah, the cruelty of it all. Yes, it peed again, red pee, kind of rust-coloured. Probably tore the tubing, allowing rust from the old pipe to bleed into the water. A perfectly logical explanation. But I felt defeated, utterly humiliated. All the improbable coincidences. Martin and his family were here when I turned it on. The girls blushed. The elder one said that David was peeing monthlies. Her father glared, her mother smiled at her daughter's cleverness. My shame burned in me that day, throughout lunch and afternoon tea and even when they had gone, like some kind of inner acid. Not in my stomach, no, in my veins.

That day the stiffness was acute. After Martin and Helena had gone, Anna rubbed my back. This led to our making love. Each day now, a gentle massage to ease the pain of my stiffness led us into exploring each other's bodies, sighs echoed in the eaves of this old house, septuagenarian noises, like an old man or woman remembering out loud some past pleasure. It was as if we were being guided . . . we would awake, as if from a trance, in unimaginable positions, and blush because of the memory of it . . . the unorthodox sex. Anna asked me to be gentle. Said that my erections were wonderful, but painful inside of her when I thrust too hard. She was considerate, almost saintly. Yet it was as if there was something new in her, a body awakening from a long dreamy sleep. I remember thinking about the Afrikaans word "los" as she lay beside me. Not loose so much as languid, relaxed. Then she held me, saying she could feel something stirring inside of me, so close was I to her.

Well, we know now what that was. The roots of another being. Something struggling to be born.

She wished she could help.

Yes, the problems with my breathing had already begun.

I am a little tired. Can we stop?

YOU DID not come today. Perhaps you noted, the last time, the woodenness in my eyes, how I struggled for breath, how I spoke in short little whispers, as if I was communicating, with myself really, in some kind of Morse code. I too am trying to understand all this. Look at my skin. As coarse and grainy as the bark of some ancient tree. The itching has stopped though. The merciful death of the skin beneath this bark. Smell the dust in the air, moistened by my exhaled breath, until everything is damp. All sorts of organisms come to life, spores grow from the walls, lichen covers the floorboards. In the kitchen and bathroom, green damp has invaded the concrete floors, licking at tiles and establishing homes in the warm vaginas of the taps.

Perhaps that's why you didn't come back. You were frightened off by the virulent forests of my dementia. You did tell me you were uncomfortable with the frank manner in which I talked about my sexual desires, the vivid descriptions of so many shattered eardrums, and how, as this "illness" slowly germinated in me, I achieved the most enormous erections. It made you restless. Legs crossed and uncrossed, eyes averted.

The modesty of lust. How strange, that of all my human attributes, my sexuality remained intact. More so than my memory, which you praised, or the way I expressed myself. A gift for words rather than innocent straight lines, you said. Perhaps it was a mistake to accept you as my therapist. Funny profession, psychotherapy. A kind of prostitution, getting paid to listen.

I wanted to ask, once or twice, why a woman like you, young, good-looking, should choose such a profession. I can imagine the stories you've had to listen to. I bet that men find a particular way of telling you their stories. We always believe that women can only be interested in our sexuality. Even trees have a certain vanity. Have you ever seen those gigantic poplars dance straight-backed like township jollers, even when there is no wind to drive them on and all that they achieve is a horrible creaking as they bend and unbend? It is because they know that some woman is looking or listening. Yes, trees have lives, inner lives, sexuality, they dream of being beautiful, of being graceful in someone's arms. No one likes being awkward and stumbly when they make love.

Yesterday a group of clapper larks paid me a visit. I'd seen them tumbling through the air, clapping their wings at the last moment to stop themselves from crashing into the earth, for the simple pleasure of it. Some of them landed in the nettling of my hair. With what ease did their little claws grapple onto the sturdiness of what I imagine must by now be a wilderness of branches! I have no mirror nearby. Even if I had, what would I see that I do not already know?

Anna is gone, even Wilhelmina, our servant. To vote she said. Imagine that. A black person, a woman voting for the first time, making her first unashamed choice. She stood at the foot of my bed, talking to me as if she was addressing some dumb force of nature. The way she talked, while she cleaned, to ornaments, patriarchal African statues, drawing them into her conversations about the strangeness of white people, how our underwear smelled . . . no, I never really, consciously thought of myself as white.

I envied Wilhelmina, was glad for her, and for myself, elated even, though politics had never moved me before. I lay there imagining . . . I too would have been able to go out and vote, openly for the first time, as a black man, a half-baked one anyway, a bushy. To join in this festival they call freedom. When I opened my eyes Wilhelmina was gone.

I know that Anna will withstand Martin, will not only ward off his evil, which I think is merely a sickness, the common cold of the soul, but actually help him to deal with its incurability. One day you should get Anna to tell you her story. Remarkable, for all the hidden pain, the secret wells of pleasure, the power of unacknowledged, unspoken thoughts, mottling the green pools of her eyes. *The* most beautiful of flaws. Disperses only when she weeps. You don't believe that I loved her—and still do—as deeply as I profess. And I loved her because she was the primordial Anna, the woman all men dream of, the unattainable Eve, the seduction of silence. One day she will learn to grasp her sorrow, speak it out loud. She will become mortal, ordinary, hardened to her grief because she has come to understand it.

As for the rest of us, we cannot transform completely. Not even myths can change those invisible roots, ingrained like ancient fossil in rock. We do not metamorphose. We merely crumble into dust. That is my triumph. I have robbed Malik of something to bury, and Martin of something to despise.

I have broken the cycle of remembrance.

Malik-ul-Mout

MALIK GATHERED the claylike remains of his brother Omar into the stained and yellowed sheet in which Omar had died. When the edges were brought together, the sheet folded into the burial shroud of a child. He carried Omar's body to the green-painted hearse parked in the street. No one could find the key to the ornate iron gate that sealed off the long driveway, overgrown with grass and weeds. So the street was blocked by vehicles, the police van, the station sergeant's car with its radio tersely transmitting messages, the mortuary van which Malik had said was not needed. None of the vehicles received as much attention as the hearse, with its moon-and-star insignia, its exotically decorated windows, the driver wearing a red fez. An unnecessary show of fancy, Malik would tell the Imam later. It makes Muslims look ludicrous.

He walked now with the slightly stooped reverence that the dead deserved, even though the body remained unpurged of the sin of its earthly smells. Malik knew that the remains were too insubstantial to withstand the munnie, the ritual cleansing Muslims performed before burying their dead. He would have to convince the Imam of the other special circumstances, that his brother Omar had renounced his Muslim name because many years ago their father brought pressure to bear on a young and impressionable boy "to survive, survive at any cost". The sins of a father should not become an obstacle in the way of a dead Muslim facing the judgement—and the consequent forgiveness—due to him. Omar's biggest sin had been his inability to accept his station in life, the takdier—the destiny—of religion, language and people into which all humans are born.

The police had summoned Malik, assuring him that they suspected no foul play, "but there was this smell, right for the neighbours to complain, and look, everyone deserves a decent burial." In any case, the rumours about the nature of his brother's death, "unnatural, people think," were attracting all kinds of strangers who came poking about and taking photographs. This was a quiet neighbourhood where nothing much hap-

pened, and the sooner the matter was laid to rest
the better.

"His wife? Whereabouts unknown."

Malik's name and telephone number had been
written down on a pad by the dead man's bedside.
The officer who spoke to Malik, with the sort of
diffidence that forced the head back and averted
the nose from an imaginary smell, was surprised
at the quick smile on Malik's serious face. Sergeant
Johnson had recently been transferred to Parkside from his small station in Paarl. There, when
the sun set on the vineyards, the workers went
home to their tidy hovels and their employers to
the brightly lit barriers of their estate homes. You
knew who and what everyone was and could
predict their little crimes. Here almost everyone
was white, even the hoboes in the park. Sarge, a
veteran of forty years, had been brought out of
retirement because he was coloured. People with
his experience were needed during the transition.

Now here was this vexing problem. This body,
this blerry body, of which there remained only
some matter, a powdery matter that crumbled at
the lightest touch, no staring eyes or gaping
mouth.

"Perhaps you want to do some forensic tests?"
Malik suggested.

A constable coughed and turned away in
embarrassment, observing out of the corner of
his eye his sergeant's guileless expression, an

open-mouthed amazement that someone of Malik's appearance, a "Bhai" in holy dress, could so confidently utter the word *forensic*. Its ring of authority questioned the many assumptions Sarge had made, assumptions the constable had endured listening to all morning.

"Just another play-white whose hidden life is being exposed, because in death we all come and claim them, our people," Sarge had said. He had seen dozens of such cases in the Cape, where blue eyes and light skins were as common as fuck, "sad really." The constable had been surprised by Sarge's easy ability to be irritated.

This one though, the constable would give anyone the odds, had other connections. "Who knows just who this dead bastard's family will turn out to be?"

He knew the case was unusual, Sergeant Johnson told Malik, but people said that they saw this *thing* happening to the dead man, like it was part of his nature. He indicated with a wave of his hand to the room, the mould on the walls, the flowers, the tree growing in the middle of the room.

"A psychologist who attended to him gave us a statement," the sergeant continued, satisfied that Malik had no explanation for the state the house was in, the strange plants, the moss and lichen climbing wildly up walls and spreading across the ceilings.

"Ja, if we really probed, the bogger's life would seem strange indeed."

66

Forensic tests would take ages, Sergeant Johnson said. There were more serious cases, serial killers, muti-murderers, street children burnt alive in their shelters, car hijackings, and all that. The police were very busy.

"In any case, I understand that you people don't like that kind of thing, cutting up bodies. A violation."

"No, we don't like that kind of thing," Malik answered.

Under the watchful eye of the police, Malik traced with his hand the skeletal outlines of a reclining, foetal shape etched into the stains of dust and sweat on the bare mattress. He grimaced, passing on his distaste to the others as they crowded around him. Malik withdrew his hand and resolved to touch nothing else, saying that the sealed and unaddressed envelope was probably intended for Omar's wife. He ignored the set of clothes, a dark suit, white shirt and red tie, the soft white kofiya, very similar to the one he wore himself, all neatly folded and displayed upon the seat of the chair.

"Ons mense begrawe nie hul dooies asof hulle op pad partytjie toe is nie," Malik said in Afrikaans, his tone mocking, but the lilt of his words so pure that everyone, the constable, the husband-and-wife neighbours who had first complained to the police about the smell, paused in their embarrassed fussing with the plants and faded carpets and dusty furniture to stare at

Malik. It was as if someone else had spoken those words, a ventriloquist hidden behind the conventional bearded Indian face that Malik wore like a mask, and this hidden manipulator now caused him to turn arrogantly on his heel and leave the rest of them stranded in that room heavy with the dust of death. None of them felt they could depart without Malik's permission.

Sergeant Johnson recognised that accent, the faint trace of smooth Slamse syrup underneath the stern Afrikaner tone. With an impatient cluck of his tongue, the sergeant led them from the bedroom, down corridors where the floors still felt stout underfoot despite the pervasive damp and decay, to the veranda where Malik stood with a sudden proprietorial air. The policeman shrugged and locked the door behind him, then turned, ready to assert custodianship of the key to the house—there were still formalities to be completed.

But Malik was walking away rapidly, past other neighbours who stood on the pavement in small groups. They knew by now that Oscar was not Oscar, the austere but friendly man who kept to himself, that his real name was Omar, though someone even said that it did not matter any more. Apartheid was gone, and people could live where they wanted. In any case, he was never a bother to anyone in the street.

"But think of the wife, think of Anna, what she

must have felt like when she discovered that he wasn't Oscar. Well, you know, that Oscar wasn't who he said he was."

Anna's disappearance had a logical explanation after all! At least he did not murder her.

"Of course that was a possibility!" One never knows what goes on in the minds of people who forsake their own kind.

Malik exchanged a few sharp words with a reporter, then climbed into the front of the hearse beside the driver.

"They have a very practical attitude towards the dead," someone who had a Muslim colleague at work said as the hearse drove off. "They don't have you hanging around the house spreading grief and, who knows, all kinds of smells."

The body, transferred into a proper calico shroud and sealed tight to prevent the oozing of sweetly smelling dust, like the decay of old flowers in the market, lay in state on the floor of Malik's living room, emptied for the second time that year to accommodate a funeral. Fatgiyah, Malik's wife, sternly rebuked the children who were invited to pray beside the body but who gawked instead at the shapeless form which, they had heard, was really a shrivelled tree.

Meanwhile, Malik spent a tedious day trying to reclaim—in legal terms—Omar Khan from Oscar Kahn. This was no easy matter, Malik discovered, so authentic were the forged alterations

to Omar's birth certificates, so real the "adop-
tive" parents, Isaac and Marian Kahn, immigrants from Britain.

"Smelled the war coming," the clerk in Home
Affairs said. He remembered that late-thirties
wave. "Not poor at all."

White shirts, soft hats, polished shoes. You
could tell from the shoes the kind of people they
were, generally speaking. Proper papers too,
most of them. No, it was impossible for any death
certificate to be issued to someone called Omar
Khan, who, according to the records, had never
existed.

"Listen, unofficial," the clerk advised, "bury
Oscar, pray for Omar. It happens all the time. No,
you forget, race does not matter any more. What
you look like won't prove anything even if you
are his brother, and we don't know that for sure,
do we? In any case, what's the difference between
Khan and Kahn? A spelling mistake?"

The burial took place the next day, at the practical hour after magrieb, the edge of time between
sunset and darkness. This allowed mourners to
attend without having to take time off from work.
A small kifayet of green hearse and four cars
wound its way rapidly from Malik's home in the
township of Newclare to the Croesus cemetery.

Imam Ismail proved wise to the ways of this
new world and prayed for Omar. In his graveside
homily he reminded fellow mourners that forgiveness was a pillar of Islam.

"Allah will judge, our task is to pray for our brother, even though he strayed from the true path. As-salaam-wa-aleikum-wa-ragmatullah," Imam Ismail said in farewell to the dead, waited for the brief, chorused rejoinder, then turned away from the grave, signalling that it was appropriate now for Omar to give answer for the sins of his life to Malik-ul-Mout. God's interrogating angel disliked the intrusion of lamenting songs or tearful voices. The sounds of earthly grief, it was said, weakened the resolve of the dead to speak honestly about their transgressions, half remembering in the cold and rapidly dissolving memory of their souls the warmth of the life they had left behind.

Imam Ismail found Malik lingering at the graveside, sorrow showing on his face for the first time. As the Imam approached, Malik very quickly regained his composure. He even managed, as they exchanged the customary greeting of hands, to slip the white envelope containing the fee into the Imam's pocket. How adept Malik was in the graces that helped to smooth the many trials faced by Muslims in this hostile world.

"How learned," Imam Ismail said approvingly, as he and other mourners were welcomed to Malik's home for a meal.

Fatgiyah waited at the gate.

"There's a woman who wants to speak to you. She knew Omar."

"Have they no respect? Let me deal with her," Imam Ismail offered.

"It may be his wife, Imam," Malik said.

"Ah, then you have a *duty* to perform," Imam Ismail said, his voice dropping to the profound whisper Imams are taught to perfect.

It was not Anna, Omar-turned-Oscar's wife, who sat in Malik's deep armchair in the study, but a younger woman—though Malik had no idea how old Anna was, remembering only a graver face, aged the way wives of restless men age. The woman stood up and extended her hand, which Malik took diffidently before seating himself, stiff and formal, in an upright chair.

"My name is Mandelstam, Amina Mandelstam," she said, aware that the uttering of her hybrid name had startled Malik. "I was Oscar's therapist. I mean Omar. You must forgive me, it is difficult to suddenly separate the image from the name."

Conscious that she had transgressed some unwritten code of authority, Amina was ready to relinquish Malik's chair, but paused in this deliberate act of diplomacy, struck by an unexpected thought.

"You know, his name, the name he took—Oscar—defined his personality. It sounds unscientific and illogical, I know, and yet . . ."

She saw in Malik's bearing that slow manly scorn, and sat down opposite him, in a chair as stiff and uncomfortable as his own. Between them the armchair rocked on its coiled springs, a troublesome, vacant throne. Malik, despite his own sense of place, lowered his eyes when confronted by Amina Mandelstam's weary submission to the patriarchal authority so evident in this household. He looked up again as she sat down, and was suddenly confronted by the fresh distraction of her exposed knees, their tightly drawn paleness under the dark stockings. Her hair was quite comfortably held in place by the fashionable scarf she wore. Muslim women—Muslim-born women at least—never forget the art of wearing scarves. It showed some sensitivity on her part, some respect for the Muslim home she was visiting.

"I'm sorry that I didn't call first. All I had was an address," she said. "Do you have a moment to speak?"

Malik recovered his authority. Something in her voice, not so much its businesslike tone, but the not-quite-American softening of once strong Capetonian vowels, made her seem foreign and intrusive.

"The kifayet has just finished, you know what that means. I have to attend to my guests."

Malik's reproach was unmistakable. Since her return from abroad, she had constantly been confronted by this disapproval of her "foreign" accent, the loss of her native gestures and intonation. She had grown weary of telling even the most intelligent among her own family that during her years away she had lived in places of exile—Dar es

Salaam, Algiers, Toronto, Paris, New York—
where she was also regarded as a foreigner
because of her accent. She no longer knew, she
told them, who "her" people were. The sadness
in her voice, the plea for understanding, was usually mistaken for bitterness, a woman unable to
take the consequences of her actions.

"You rejected us and our culture, and now you
want understanding from us?" their silent faces
always seemed to say. She could not bring herself
to tell "her" people that she had lived with her
husband in Israel, or openly acknowledge that
her husband was Jewish.

"Can I make an appointment for another
time?"

"What is it about? No point in making ap-
pointments if there's nothing to discuss."

His abruptness was unusual though. Normally
she encountered a patronising politeness, especially from men. Mister Khan was like his brother,
forthright at least in his folly.

"Mr Khan, I counselled your brother for a
whole year. He was making good progress, then
I had to go away—personal reasons—and when
I returned, just days ago, I found out he was
dead."

Malik was tempted to ask what the personal
reasons for her departure had been, for she said
this with so much concealed meaning that he
knew her mind had momentarily strayed to a
matter not connected to her visit here, that there

was now in her a new tension, her composure forced and fragil.

"There was nothing unnatural about his death, was there? The police tell me they don't suspect anything."

"Yes, yes, I don't mean that there's anything to suspect. It's just that his relapse was so sudden."

Amina Mandelstam stood up, ready to leave. She knew that she was arousing a curiosity in Malik about things he was unlikely to understand or have sympathy for. His face had the same look of implacable patience as Oscar's when he debated an idea she had raised, besieging it on all sides with incisive but contradictory forces of examination, until the concept she had suggested as a means of dealing with his problems was left in tatters. Elated by the discussion, Amina often ignored the fact that she was being defeated, that her professional ability to contend with Oscar Kahn's devious personalities had diminished with each session. It was undeniable: he had made remarkable progress, and very often seemed more lucid than she, not by being faithful to the progressive methods she had been taught, but by subverting them.

Far from ridding himself of his delusions and their torment by coming to terms with their illusory nature, he had brought them to life, often with her collusion. Once, they had been discussing the recurring dreams he had of his grandmother's nakedness. In the middle of his description of her ageing body, Oscar had stood up and walked over to Amina, touched her gently on the neck and said, "She has a tiny scar on her right breast, like a crescent moon, in exactly the same spot you have your scar. Yours is round. Like a full moon." He had run his hand down her throat to her breast, touched her nipple for a moment, then resumed his seat. Amina had not rebuked him. She remembered now the feeling of great, clear lust that overcame her for as brief a moment as Oscar had touched her breast. His dream had not recurred after that, or at least he had never spoken about it again.

Oscar had said that Malik always saw things in simple black-and-white terms, that he did not believe in ambiguities, a reaction against their father who had lived his whole life balancing dozens of ambiguities. Malik disliked people who lived by their wits, and as a consequence reacted strongly against those who held no definitive positions and beliefs.

"Mrs Mandelstam, Omar is dead and buried."

Amina realised that she had been standing in silence before Malik for some time, allowing him to observe and assess her, the very same way Oscar used to, taking advantage of the silence that she told him was legitimate and even necessary at times. She noticed a bemusement in Malik's eyes which would soon bring a smile to her face and force her to sit down again, slumped and ungainly. She had only recently learned that

Malik Khan was an important figure in the new political establishment, a member of the Provincial Legislature. And no fool, that much she could see. She was not sure whether he had actually asked or whether she had imagined him asking if it was not correct that her real concern was the failure of the science that she practised, that Omar's illness had defied the logic of Western thought because the illness was one of the spirit, a condition that was not mere primitive hocus-pocus?

No, she answered herself silently. In all truth—kassamtie, the childhood oath to God's truth came to her mind—that was not her only concern. There had been a deeper bond between Oscar and herself. A relationship yes, not physical, but a relationship of words, carefully spun words, as well as spontaneous outpourings, evasions and confessions. Silent tears, for neither of them could bear to cry openly, and silences, silences that were the most intimate of all the unspoken intimacies. He understood my loneliness, the terror of unbelonging. Finally, and still without having spoken, she rummaged in her bag and found a business card which she handed to Malik.

"Please call me when you find some time."

Malik ushered her out into the wintry street. Smog hid the township behind a thin blue veil.

"Lock your doors," he cautioned as she climbed into her car.

Malik returned to his living room, which was filled with the peaceful murmur of familiar voices, to join his fellow mourners in their communal meal. Omar in his cold grave would by now be giving account for his deeds. We all do, one way or another. Most of us would be called to account very formally, to an angel's inquisition, once we were dead and in our graves. But the unlucky ones would have to give answer to the living and to life itself. Judgement after death was not the only punishment that god imposed on sinners. Poor Omar, how he must have suffered during his lifetime, just consider the people he got mixed up with. Malik ate with nimble fingers from the steaming plate a young server brought to him, aware that most of the mourners were there because of him rather than out of any real sorrow for Omar's death.

But these were his people and this their generosity, unwilling to judge, publicly at least, even those apostates who renounced their names and their religion. Amina Mandelstam. What a name to have to carry through life. At least Omar chose a name that did not jar: "Oscar" had the same ring to it as "Omar". But Amina Mandelstam? What an aberration. That's what these bastard unions create. Malik realised that he was muttering to himself and dismissed the sudden memory of Amina's taut knees. Omar was dead and buried. Malik was not about to open any wounds, not for anyone's sake. His people called it fietna. The supreme form of mischief-making.

"She's as thin as a white woman," Malik's daughter Rabia said, sensing her father's preoccupation with the intruder.

Many eyes admonished the young woman, not so much for what she had observed, but for her temerity at answering out loud the question that others in the room may have had in their minds. Was that woman white or black, a non-believer in a believer's scarf?

When the funeral was over, Malik locked away the soiled sheet in which he had borne home Omar's body. Then he went about his life as before, tending to the needs of his constituents in the western part of Johannesburg, attending meetings to combat crime and drugs, arguing in the legislature for more services and more police and more lights in those townships where gangs ruled the darkness, until he was nicknamed Comrade Hajji More. He was a good debater, entertaining in the manner in which he derided the opposition—"the baadjievangers of history", those who ride on history's coattails—and there was always a sizeable audience in the gallery when he was scheduled to speak. Once, he saw Amina Mandelstam among the brown faces who loved to hear him talk about their plight, but quickly dismissed her and her mangled name and recovered in mid-sentence the flow of his speech.

He went, happily for the most part, about the practice of power. His white djellaba, worn summer and winter, swish-swished defiantly in the dull, brown-stone corridors where other leaders of the revolution acquired a studious sameness, blue shirts and red ties and black shoes that squeaked from their newness. His steadfast adherence to his religion and its customs—he never attended meetings on Thursday nights or during the Juma prayer hour on Fridays, no matter how urgent—created a confidence in him, even within the primarily Christian coloured community which he represented. Malik Khan was a symbol of simple honesty, even among his opponents who had called him Koelie-Khan during the bitter election campaign.

Our people love the exotic, there's a bit of the pagan in us, they said good-humouredly.

FATGIYAH WAS a gleeful deliverer of bad tidings. She would stand at their tiny gate, which was of the rare kind that people were still able to lean over, to await Malik's arrival and inform him of a death in the family, a relative's unwelcome visit, some disruption or other to the calm haven that Malik hoped his home would be in the midst of a hectic life. He had expanded the modest cottage, an impoverished remnant salvaged by his father from the ruins of a black-marketeering empire, until the house occupied almost every inch of the land. Malik was thus able to separate his and Fatgiyah's sleeping quarters from those of their children, and their living space from Malik's working space. Above all, he was able to create a small sanctuary isolated from the rest of the house.

Malik retired each night to this tiny room which could only be reached by going through his study, a trespass that neither wife nor child dared commit. The sanctuary had been cleared of all furniture except for a small lectern meant for the Holy Book. Seated on cushions, Malik read passages from his favourite philosophers, allowing the many ideas they evoked to flow through his mind, reverence converging with irreverence, the Sufi Yusuf Ali and the heretic Tariq Ali, a turbulent babble of tongues and musings. At the end, he pictured in his mind a waterfall gleaming with the dark effluent of discarded thought, until he felt emptied of all contemplation or emotion.

After many hours of sitting in a cramped position, gently swaying to and fro as the faithful do in prayer, he would struggle to his stiff legs and walk like an old man to their bedroom where Fatgiyah lay awake, her resentment carefully concealed by her stately breathing. She no longer hoped that he would reach out to her, even with his cold and bitter limbs, that the blood returning to his starved veins would allow him the generosity of an embrace, or a smile at the very least, some acknowledgement of her presence and her humanity. Sex was what he took when his body urged its need on him. This, too, was as cold as it was fierce, and mercifully occurred with less and less frequency. Most often, he fell immediately into a deep sleep, lying on his back without moving, his face empty and serene. When he awoke in the morning there was in him the renewed innocence of a child. Fatgiyah, overcome by an emotion she could not understand and that she would loathe herself for later on, accepted as endurable, if only for one more day, the loneliness that her life of devotion to her husband pressed on her like an unwanted gift.

This allegiance was not formally taught, was no dogma that their religious instructors impressed on young girls in madressa. Fatgiyah had learned the skilful art of conquered emotions from her mother and elder sister, had acquired from other women the serenity of concealed desires, hiding behind headscarves and kurtas the unutterable beauty that, she thought, could only be explored in the secrecy of darkened bedrooms. Lust, even between husband and wife, was so immodest an emotion that they dared not look upon each other's nakedness for fear of acknowledging its power over them, thereby incurring God's wrath. Children conceived in lust were doubly flawed, doomed to suffer that moment of sin between their parents in addition to the other natural, inborn sins of greed, envy and ambition. Lust, she learned, was too strong a word for a woman, for in the eyes of men it turned women's natural desires "makroef", made them a perversion.

So Fatgiyah waited for her husband to reach out across the expanse of dark expectation that the space between them in bed gradually became, until she learned to fall asleep despite the disconsolate needs of her own body. The feeling that the slow, patterned tread of her life was in her husband's hands at first filled her with the peace of a destiny fulfilled. This "good" man, this "prominent" man, this man whom she had married after a watched-over courtship, had at least a cold wisdom to distinguish him from the dull eyes of other, rejected suitors from her youth, all with wives of their own now upon whom they could thrust their blunt tyranny. Fatgiyah, her childhood friends said, had made the best choice.

"Ah, yes, the joy that Islam brings to Muslims," someone would offer, careful not to betray any resentment of Malik's eminent position in their community, but nevertheless with sly benevolence attributing Fatgiyah's "luck" to God rather than Malik. Such compliments, paid in public by men and women alike, desperate to believe in the serenity of their lives, in defiance of a world that regarded their traditions as outdated or even oppressive, brought a blush of pride to Fatgiyah's face, a pleasure marred only by Malik's scornful attitude.

"Islam does not need to feed off our vanity."

She laughed at the suggestion that men like Malik were destined to betray their wives, dismissing hints that there may already be another woman in his life. "My poor, always-tired husband? He doesn't even have the energy for one!"

Yet, despite her outward tranquillity there slowly grew in the placid soil of Fatgiyah's soul a discontent which drove her to the gate of their home in the evenings, where she would lean over its edge, waiting to tell Malik that all was not well in the sanctuary he was trying to create.

"There is a bird in the house."

"A bird? What kind of bird?"

There was an utter weariness in his voice, a tone that said, *This has been a trying day, please save until tomorrow, until another time, your misfortunes, however terrible they may seem right now, they will disappear or diminish as the night goes by, as we eat our supper and talk as a family, and you in the end will do the things that bring you peace and I will do mine.* Undeterred, Fatgiyah stood aside to offer her husband the welcome of an open gate, all the while guiding him to the defect in his citadel of peace, before he had time to subside into an impenetrable silence.

"A big bird . . . and ugly . . . came in through the kitchen door with ugly cries, haa! haa!"

Malik looked around to see whether there were any passers-by in the street, for he had a position to uphold. How cruel his people could be with their rancidly honeyed tongues. He imagined them dubbing him "Mad Fats's man".

"Flapped its wings and shrieked at us. Poor Rabia is in such a state."

"Where is it now?"

"In your 'bacha' room. Strutted right through the house."

Malik deposited his briefcase, as was his custom, beside the hallway table, but did not pick up the mail. He was disturbed, and would not slide just yet into the icy quiet that overcame him each night. Normally, he walked towards his study, glancing at letters and messages, passing them from one hand to the other, the concerns of the day settling in him like the shadows outside, a colourless dusk of self-containment. In his study, he would seat himself in the huge, creaking armchair, smilingly receive Rabia's kiss on his cheek, and even on occasion enquire after his son Fadiel. The moment the door shut he would be lost to his family, emerging only to share a subdued dinner. He ate slowly, chewing his food as thoroughly as the ideas being ground over in his mind.

Now, sensing his bewilderment at the bird's strange and unwelcome intrusion, Fatgiyah pressed home the sharpened edge of the many unsaid things that passed between them.

"This would not have happened if Fadiel was home."

She knew that she had touched some wounded

part of Malik's memory, that this ritual hour of solitary reflection, during which he recomposed all the jagged fragments of the things he could not control, was being threatened. She was not supposed to broach such sensitive subjects now, there was a time and place even for tragedy.

"Why Fadiel?"

"Because he would have been here, a man to help me."

Fatgiyah hoped to touch Malik's sense of patriarchy, to fill him with the horror of a father's duty not done. Fadiel had dropped out of university and was living in some kind of commune in Kalk Bay, a dirty fishing village outside Cape Town. People whispered to her, "Your son is addicted to dagga, he lives like a wild Rasta, his hair, did you see his hair, twisted into dreadies? And there's this white woman, she must've put a dinges in his tea. Ja-nee, all the chicken-licken that these wit bokkies give up, better than our women? No Muslim lives like that. Do something!"

She no longer repeated to her husband these tales of a dreadlocked Fadiel and the woman with the whore's-gold down of hair on her sunburnt legs—"It's their nakedness, Allah maaf!"—tales embroidered with the glorious indelicacy of tongue-clicking gossip, passed down a chain of friends and acquaintances, distant cousins, aunts deserted by their husbands, and a sequence of uncles, who suddenly discovered their famous relative, Salaam Fuck-up's son, Malik the politician.

"They make fietna, like shrews. How close do you think they have to look, these faithful Muslim men," he often retorted in his lecturing-learned-man manner, "to see a woman's private hair stick out of her underwear?"

"A bikini it was, they saw," Fatgiyah had responded wearily, knowing that he would stride away, leaving her tangled in the threads of an unfinished story. Now, she recognised the advantage provided by the bird's prophetic invasion of their home. "Maybe this is an omen, a message. Allah has strange ways of telling us things."

At the door to his sanctuary, Malik hesitated for a moment, ready to turn on Fatgiyah, full of scorn and disdain. Later she would have to breach this surly barrier with a false humility that shamed them both, but that at least allowed life to continue, their peacemaking tacit, the cause of their rift unacknowledged.

But there before them stood the bird, its spindly-legged, black-beaked ugliness blocking Malik's path. The bird seemed to her to have grown in size, its malevolence filling the sacred prayer room.

Haa! haa! the bird screamed as soon as Malik and Fatgiyah moved, until it trapped them into immobility, uttering, after each foray and resistance, more subdued but no less strident warning cries—Ha! Ha-de-da!—and flapping its huge wings. Malik observed a gash under one of the wings, where blood gleamed on its undelicious down. Suddenly, he had found a logical explanation for the bird's presence, a way of managing the threat to the equilibrium of his home and his ritual rest-hour. He whispered to Fatgiyah that the thing was in pain.

"Scaring it doesn't help. It just makes it more frantic."

The room was dark and cool, and perhaps the bird felt safe in there.

"Let's go," he said loudly, suddenly conscious of his absurd, conspiratorial whisper. He left the study door open and, with some effort, pushed back the large window on hinges eroded by rust. The air was filled with the smell of antique decay, noises from the street invaded the tranquil atmosphere of books and Bibles, Torah and Koran translated into eleven languages, most of which Malik could not understand but which brought even to his Spartan mind a sense of learnedness. The bird renewed its cries of raucous triumph. Far from being distressed by the unexpected assault of dusty smells and brittle noise, Malik felt calmed by their familiarity. These were the odours and sounds of his childhood. Late afternoon, a thronging, township peacefulness of people returning from work, starting fires, cooking, cleaning, doing the things their working lives allowed them to do while the sun was still up.

Soon the blue security lights—already beginning their osmosis with the slow darkness—would be a glaring reminder that the night belonged to blue-coated policemen and their antagonists, lounging in tenement stairwells like cats tautly stretched on slender spinal hooks. Even then, there was about the place the guarded welcome of softer light, flowing like music from the windows onto the darkened streets.

As for this bird—he observed in the semi-darkness the dull sparkle of its eyes, the only mark of an indolent beauty—it too was not unique. It came, merely, from another darkness like this one. Malik remembered seeing such birds in the garden of Omar's house near the Zoo Lake. A number of them, two, three—he remembered only that they seemed such a fittingly funereal flock—had landed on the lawn the day he went to fetch Omar's body. They pecked at the grass with sharp, practised beaks, impervious to the gloomy group of onlookers waiting, like Malik, for the police to finish their business. "It's related to the Sacred Ibis," one of them had remarked, noticing his curiosity.

He would tell Fatgiyah none of this, though, for he knew that she was ready once more to exploit the bird's presence, to endow on this trivial event a deeper meaning and use it to engage him in discussion about their son, about Rabia's future. Or she would launch into an analysis of her own misery, speaking in the most gentle of voices, the deferential tone a weapon in itself. No, Fatgiyah did not believe in omens, unlike many foolish people who confused faith with a lack of logic. Fatgiyah used sooth-saying and vision-seeing as a device to achieve some very practical ends.

Throughout their silent dinner Malik retained his mask of pained austerity. Rabia's girlish chatter subsided into a resentful soliloquy, loudly scratching knife and fork against plate as she ate, in punishment for their own muteness. Even as they made ready for bed they did not speak. Robbed of the privacy of his prayer room, he sat in a chair in their bedroom, observing his wife remove mascara from her eyes, astonished by the nakedness that this left in her face, by the nakedness of her body, its remarkable firmness, the darkness of her skin. He shut his eyes and had a distant, pleasurable recollection of the coarse-silk down of hair, black as river-edge reeds, that covered her body. She was like a stranger, wondrously forbidden, a pornographic photograph observed with an ephemeral desire.

They slept uneasily that night, disturbed by Fatgiyah's restlessness. Her concern for Fadiel, and Malik's intractable resolution to "let the boy find out for himself what life was like" tortured her, until her body itched all over and she was forced to rise and bathe herself, the water anointed with moisturising oils. It was this ghostly sensuality, as she lay in the bath, a candle

providing the only light, for she did not want to
disturb Rabia who sensed bright lights being
switched on even in her sleep, that finally made
Fatgiyah decide to leave Malik. A vague idea
which shaped itself, found colour and form in the
pale flickering flame hissing urgently as moisture
settled on its wick.

She understood—a new, burdensome wisdom—that she and her husband had not merely
drifted apart, that this would be too easy an explanation for the alienation between them. Earlier
that night Malik had watched her with the eyes of
a stranger, a voyeur whose sight had been dulled
into indifference by the relentless observation of
naked flesh. This did not shock her. She knew
that the many solitary hours Malik spent in his
silent room, the many years of withdrawal into
privately demarcated corners of crowded family
spaces had not been in pursuit of God or even in
contemplation of the writings of heretic philosophers, but were a way of continuing to imprison
inside of himself the many temptations demanded
by an evil seed, a Magog licking away at the thin
walls that separated Malik-the-Sanguine from his
father Salaam-the-Sly and his grandfather Shaik-
the-Sadistic.

"It is in their genes, their drunken genie, he
drives them mad . . . ships short of their mooring," Nazier, Malik's second cousin, said when
news was heard of Omar's strange death. "Of
course, it affects only the direct male line,"

Nazier had added, protesting his immunity. "My grandmother Mariam—thank God for her dungs—used to frighten us with her bogeyman brother Shaik, who cut himself to see what blood looked like. Imagine what he would have done to naughty children!"

Oh, the murmured scandal, the eyes-averted knowingness whenever the name of Ouma Kulsum, Malik's grandmother, was mentioned. She loved, it was said, her own son Salaam too much, too closely, too physically. And after him, her grandson Malik. Fatgiyah remembered the stories about how Ouma Kulsum, who conceived Salaam before she was fifteen, could not suckle the infant when he was born. Her breasts, a pair of unripe melons, seemed frozen in childlike beauty. A woman who had just given birth was searched out. A servant, one of Shaik's concubines, a squatter in one of Johannesburg's backyards—who knows with this family?—was forced to breastfeed Salaam while her own child screamed from hunger. Ouma Kulsum used to stuff wax into her ears so as not to hear the deprived baby's wailing.

Then, when Malik was born he also was taken away from his mother Salma—what a taste for child-women these Khan men had—her breasts too young to feed her first child. Ouma Kulsum, intoxicated by the baby's sweet breath, his first straight-out-of-the-womb gurgle of oxygen, took the child, intending perhaps to find another poor woman desolate enough to sell her breast-milk, but ended up nestling Malik between her own sterile little beauties. Miracle of miracles. Ouma Kulsum's tits swelled with milk that tasted musty, like the condensed syrup she had stolen as a child from her own parsimonious mother's hoard of tinned food. So strong, so constant was Ouma Kulsum's lactation, that after Malik had drunk his fill she was able to dispatch bottles of fresh breast-milk to the starving infants of mal-nourished women in the shacks of the township. Perhaps she remembered with guilt and remorse how she had starved another child to feed her own. More likely she didn't want to owe anyone anything. Ouma Kulsum always paid her debts.

Malik remained the only male ever to caress with his lips Ouma Kulsum's purpled nipples or to rest his head in the freckled-stone crevice between her breasts. Not even Shaik was permit-ted to touch this part of her body, which had become the haven of her womanhood.

"You cannot compete with what Malik sucked," a withered aunt—they constantly ap-peared from nowhere, a shadowy supply of rel-atives, attracted to the honeyed flower of sin that the Khans represented—told Fatgiyah. Perhaps she was right. Only once did Malik gaze, for a few moments, upon Fatgiyah's breasts, then curtly told her to cover them up, "They hang like old fruit."

Ouma Kulsum on her deathbed had breasts as

firm as a twenty-year-old's, full and luminous, even though the rest of her body was wizened and her hair had turned completely grey. Then there was the story of a Mr Chow who, at a drunken mah-jong game, described the crescent scar on Kulsum's breast. He was found days later, his throat slit vertically from chin to Adam's apple, so that babbling blood flowed back into wheezing vocal cords. Imam Ismail's predecessor, Sheg-Sleg Haroon, was said to have touched Kulsum's breasts of youth as he helped to wash her body, and died a similar death, long after Shaik had put a gun into his own mouth to taste what darkness was like.

Fatgiyah stroked with her fingers the soft, untangled lengths of hair rising from her skin, floating and swaying on the surface of the bath water. Even this remarkable, hirsute gift was incapable, she knew, of satisfying Malik's need to suffer love obsessively.

MALIK DID not dream so much as remember in his sleep. Smells especially, so that in his waking hours he sniffed his body, as if trying to conjure the odour of a remembrance. Malt-and-yeast-and-brown-sugar heat in Ouma's room above Mr Dada's spice-shop in the poorest part of Newclare. The sun caught in the mist of dust rising from bags of unrefined malt. Using an ancient scale, Oupa Shaik poured more-or-less correct

proportions of the ingredients for illicit home-
brewed beer into brown-paper bags. Ouma Kulsum was next in the production line, adding a
cake of yeast and a block of precut hops. Aaron—
the cleverest fingers, the quickest eyes a man can
have—sealed the bags with a juggler's swift
rustle and stacked them inside a cardboard box
on which was stencilled in large black letters
FRAGILE—EGGS. Aaron would later deliver
these consignments of potent "eggs" to Shaik's
customers, rich shebeen queens and poor immigrant Mosotho women who used the packages
to create their own deadly skokiaan variations,
spiked with cheap wine or brandy, or methylated
spirits if the fancy took them, even the occasional
amaChina hard liquor bootlegger who wanted to
diversify his business by attracting "darkie-beer"
customers.

For many years, long after Salaam shed the
bastard-child's animal softness and grew into
sleek manhood, Kulsum kept this room over the
shop, simply furnished and scrubbed clean, as a
refuge where she sat pondering, perhaps, the
moment her fate changed its course, when
Katryn the young Afrikaner girl slept with Shaik
the son of the chili-smous—it was for love, his
smooth skin and sentinel penis, Katryn's doos of
flaming red hair, his bit of money and her poverty
had nothing to do with it—when Katryn became
the "koelie-hoer" and was driven out by her family. She wept for her family's impoverished

shame, the portent of death she saw in her father's anguished eyes, wept as her young girl's dignity was stripped from her along with her clothes, when Shaik's mother seized her as she would a child to wash out the lice the old woman was sure nested in Katryn's gold-dirt hair.

"Oh, what will we call you?" Shaik's father lamented, "a Muslim girl must have a name that God recognises." He summoned a black-bearded dwarf who snipped a length of Katryn's glistening, petroleumed locks and whispered in her ear the quick and merciless ritual of rebirth, "Kulsum, daughter of faith."

Katryn-turned-Kulsum wiped the snot of her tears from her face with the sleeve of an ornate white dress, garlanded in braids of gold.

"Oh Salim, what balaa this son of yours, this Shaik son-of-a-donkey has brought to our house!"

Shaik's rage when he returned from a business trip, God knows what business and where, was mother-defiling and father defying.

"All I ask is for you to look after her and look what you've done! Turned my Kattie into an onnie-wearing little Guji mouse. Leave my wife alone, or jaar! I'll kill you both."

Shaik's father Salim, the last of a short line of sane Khans, found solace in Katryn's conversion, enforced though it was. Her metamorphosis from Katryn-white-kaffir who did not wash her arse to

Kulsum-the-pure, invested with white-scarved chasteness, would bring another moment's holy reward in heaven.

Shaik's mother and father—Kulsum could never recall the woman's name—both died of broken hearts even before Salaam was born. Shaik's madness, old Salim discovered in his ponderously vigilant way, was caused by the Devil's brew, dagga and alcohol. "He drinks, this son of mine, smokes majat, and oh Lord, sin of all sins, sells it, to make money from the kafier's misery!"

"I will never work in another koelie-bhai's shop!" Shaik said, flinging down before his father a bundle of notes. "Enough to buy us freedom from your bondage to Mr Dada."

Shaik's wealth though was fragile, with more invested than returned, as is the nature of all illicit commerce. Especially when Old Mr Dada, who had paid for Salim Khan's passage from India by contracting him and his heirs into the shop-counter service, bribed the police, those hairy sister-fuckers who did any-job-for-ten-bob, to raid and harass and make miserable Shaik and his whore and their child, who laughed like Iblis, the Devil himself, lived inside of him.

Soon Kulsum's lair became the Wit-Bok's knop-joint, or the Koelie-hoer's poes-palace, depending on the observer's prejudice, where many men were said to have been seared for ever by the fiery temple of her sexuality, a "cunt of fire" raised upon a bier of red hair in a long and sinewy confluence of pale legs somewhat misshapen by concentration-camp rickets.

Mr Chow, the fah-fee king and miller's agent; menial Aaron, Shaik's street agent, still covered in the coarse dust of the malt that he hawked; Sergeant Swart Vark Rossouw, who it is said spat on Kulsum when he was finished with his fuck, but kept his white-man's word and freed Koelie-Shaik who had been caught in possession of intoxicating ingredients "for the purpose of profit". All who took advantage of Kulsum's plight were branded with the blush of shame, their faces darkening with the mark of a corrupted Cain, whenever Kulsum glanced at them. Her eyes never lost their hatred.

Ouma Kulsum had her way of telling of things.

"As poor as thin-man's shit, as tight as poor-man's belt. We made our money by selling kaffir-beer kits to kaffirs poorer than us. Charity se moer. The only charity we ever got, your Pa and me, was a kick in the arse. And that hurts . . . you wait and see."

Soon the money they made bought them an exiled respectability in a slum better than the one they started in, a house in a new-style "native township". Ouma refused to give up the room above Mr Dada's spicery. As reward for her devotion to him, Shaik, who had already paid off his father's debt to Mr Dada, now bought out the merchant and boarded up his spice-shop.

Kulsum, rocking in her chair, read books in Afrikaans, listened to music that did not seem fitting for her home, smiling sadly when it was time to go. In the sealed-up shop below, abandoned spices (ingredients for Gujarati curries and medicinal balms) were stirring; pungent dhunia leaves found solace in beds of red-leaved wara-bhaji spinach; baked by shafts of secret sun, kalonji onion seeds burst, their combustion soothed by char-magaj melon pips; illicit unions of fruit and flower, fenugreek and tymol, nelaphany root and sprouted moong gave metamorphic birth to virile mongrel species of spice, each emitting a sweet scent of horror at lives so darkly conceived.

This was Malik's offence: the ability to divine sorrows concealed. He smelled the omens of life and death beneath the surface of things, the calcified lumps in the skin of the psyche. Ouma never did tell Oupa Shaik where the money came from to buy more stock, or why a man as ruthless as Mr Chow was willing to wait for his money, or why the police eventually left them in hateful abeyance. No, he would not have understood, the ryk-mister-kaalgat that he was. She glared at Malik in whom at first she found silent and unobtrusive company. No, his eyes said. He knew, Oupa Shaik knew. This was *his* madness.

About to leave her room above the whorehouse of the world, she fixed her hair and addressed her son Salaam, his image imagined in the mirror beginning to blotch at the edges. "Remember, only rats work to eat, to survive. Do it to make progress. Don't be a ryk-mister-kaalgat all your life." Salaam's gravely summoned image did not seem fully to understand. But Malik did. This utilitarian gift, the ability to put beauty to use, to subject loveliness to the same measure as an artisan's sure hands or the unyielding calculus of a usurer's mind, was imposed upon Kulsum at a very early age, and brought with it its own unforgiving burdens of inner strength. Not once, ever, so she believed, had anyone loved her for the sheer sake of it. A touch, no matter how deeply intimate, was saved from vulgarity because of its spontaneity, a simple gesture to celebrate beauty. Her beauty. Except perhaps the first time, with Shaik. No, even then there was some premeditation, a daring on his part, the bravado of defying society and its gods, defying even God Himself. She remembered the vow he had made to God, confessed to her in one of his rare fragile moments: "I will not take a woman until I am rich. I swore this to God on the Koran." A desperate, child's vow, easily forgiven, easily forgotten. But he had not forgotten, and this betrayed the purity of his lust, blemished the image of his young, sweat-bathed face above her, agonised in his pleasure and agonising over hers.

Just as well. To owe nothing, to owe no one. And yet, how it would have enabled her to love like that again, without the profit of someone gained, a marriage sealed or even a love bond established. Just the freedom of having loved, without thought . . . again? Why again? It hadn't happened, ever, not even with . . .

Instinctively, Malik saw in his child's mind how Ouma Kulsum was struggling with some intrusive thought, a corrosive memory eating away at the walls of her defences, the stern-mouthed, hard-eyed exterior of an Ouma whom he loved, and loved because he feared. The pale shadow on Kulsum's sun-browned face, lipstick reapplied with anaesthetic thoroughness, an aftertaste dispelled. Hands that smoothed her forbidden breasts, touched with quick distaste her sunken belly, the irresistible sag of thighs.

"What are you looking at, you kleine kak?"

Her voice gruff and old. She stopped taking Malik along on the visits to her "property", the half-derelict shop with its smell of unbrewed beer and errant spice, walls sweating like a fearful man. It broke her heart when Salaam sold it for a song.

"Salaam, they want it for a whore-house."

"So what, Mama? Listen, there's rats in the shop underneath, it smells like a koelie bazaar. They'll simply condemn the place and break it down."

She listened to his voice, the agitation it had begun to acquire, but acknowledged the deferential tone in his rationalisation. She had urged him to be ruthless in his business deals, not to be sentimental. "In business there's the koeksisters and those who eat them." She recognised in Salaam his father's obsession with money, not its posessions, heaven knows he spent it as quickly as he made it, but a grand delirium with winning. She sensed in her son's seething mood the advent of a great gamble, an idea which intrigued him because of the risk, the intricacy of its execution. The money to be made—or lost—was incidental. This notion that money was a mere tool had ruined Shaik.

One day a detective came to the door looking for one Rehman "Raymond" Enunu, Turkish immigrant, who owned a liquor store in the centre of town. Enunu it seemed had no money of his own but owed plenty all over the show. The business's minority shareholding was registered in the name of one Salaam Khan. The policeman showed a photograph of Enunu—"He ducks and dives like a drake"—to a mute Salma and silent Kulsum. Then he shook his head as the two women shook theirs, "God, you're all ducking and diving."

The photograph, Kulsum warned her son, was of Yusuf, another of Salaam's useless layabout cousins, always in search of easy money.

"What are you up to Sal? Be careful, the Boere have been after you for a long time," she said. No, Ouma Kulsum had not forgotten she was a boeremeisie once, but it seemed that Salaam had. "I know my people. We're not dealing with Swart

Vark Rossouw. This is a new breed Sal, grey suits
and grey eyes. You can see hell in them."

Soon the duck-and-dive cop was back, looking
for a Jelal "Jimmy" Salik, another turk, owner of
a dry-goods business of which Salaam Khan was
minority shareholder. Salik was up to his neck in
ceded debt to Khan, a well-known koelie crook,
the detective would bet. And then two fugitive Lebanese emerged, "Georgie" Khoury and
"Bennie" Said, who owned a grocery store and a
taxi business respectively. And guess you what,
Khan owns half the business and they owe him
everything else. "Now, you look like a reasonable
woman," Duck-and-Dive said to Kulsum, peering closely at her cold blue eyes, "this Mr Khoury
speaks Afrikaans, after only three months in the
country. You think that's fantastic?"

Finally, one Anwar "Andy" Bey, a "Turk"
newly arrived from Istanbul, was arrested for
running fah-fee, caught red-handed with all the
numbers and the money in a shebeen where he'd
stopped off for a dop.

"He was on his way to the Chinaman, a Turkish fah-fee runner, how fantastic. Well, he sang,
loony tunes," Duck-and-Dive said triumphantly,
addressing Ouma Kulsum pointedly, "and we
didn't even have to play him the hot music. Not
one little shove, even."

Anwar "Andy" Bey, alias Abram Bhamjee,
told the police of Salaam's "proxy businessman"
swindle. He shipped poor relatives and friends to

Turkey and Lebanon, which were "European" countries with "white" citizens, and brought them back as legal immigrants, complete with identity documents, fake families and affected accents. Salaam set them up as owners, as fifty-one per cent shareholders, of businesses he bought in white areas, where the real money was. They signed letters of debt to repay money they would never even see.

Salaam was led away in handcuffs, spent a few days in jail, everyone knew this would happen, but he would wriggle out of it, you watch. He paid a huge fine, had all the businesses confiscated. They've ruined him at last. Oh, the shame of it. The case of Salaam the Boss Maker, who tried to subvert the country by "koelifying" the white race, was even raised in Parliament.

The mistake was their nicknames, Salaam confided to a friend. They took it too seriously, began to think of themselves as real businessmen. Imagine Yusuf, poor Joe-fart grandly going about calling himself "Raymond" and trying to do big deals with big businessmen. Yusuf should have sat back and enjoyed the bonsella life Salaam had planned for him.

Why the nicknames?

Added a touch of class.

Ouma Kulsum's mumbo-jumbo conversion to Islam found a new fervour. She filled her days reading aloud from the Koran, which she could not understand, its inscrutable music her solace.

She frightened Omar with tales of a vengeful
God waiting to destroy with shafts of lightning
"blerry naughty little boys". She began to hate
Malik for his disregard of her divinely inspired
gospel of pagan punishment to all those who did
not believe absolutely in God's dreadfulness.
And she fumed when Salma's brothers—Salaam
attended mosque only on the Prophet's birth-
day—described how their favourite nephew
Malik had fallen asleep during prayer on Lailatul-
Kadir, the holiest of Ramadan nights, filling the
air with an angelic sweetness which earned him
not the reprimand they had expected, but praise
from the Imam: "This is the true peace of Islam,
the innocence of a child's sleep."

"He will bring death to the world, this Malik-
Malaika of yours," Ouma said scornfully, addressing her son Salaam, while Salma's brothers
shook their heads and took their leave, their
gloating—"She's cracking up, we've been telling
Salaam"—concealed in their hushed goodbyes.

"See how Iblis smiles," Ouma Kulsum added,
as a distraught Salma carried her son to his bed.
By now Ouma Kulsum had acquired the ability to
mimic holy wisdom, to quote bright snatches of
Arabic, sayings and quotations she heard others
use. She kissed, as if they were hallowed scrip-
tures, the Arabic newspapers which Salaam had
subscribed to with a view to expanding his by
now failed swindle—"Have you seen how white
some of these Saudis and Syrians look?"

"See, Ouma's kissing the comics!" Malik would say with tears of laughter in his eyes.

Ouma Kulsum was the household taskmaster. Everybody had to do something, even young Omar, this was Ouma's nature, *her* Boere nature she used to say with malicious pride. Even though the house was filled with servants who cleaned and carried, washed and waited, Magogo imposed the lessons of poverty and servitude on her grandchildren (to the servants' bewildered delight; Magogo's loose screw was just what the country needed). Malik was assigned the most menial and punishing of tasks: cleaning up Spotty's shit from the backyard. Spotty was a township mongrel without a spot, a prodigious shitter that practically fulfilled Ouma's threat of summoning a hound from hell to punish "this evil child". It shat even as Malik cleaned, so that the boy went round in a circle, scooping, with increasing difficulty, the fresh turds that smeared the shovel, and swallowing his nausea. He refused to complain, even though the rage in his heart, which soon turned his sweet breath bitter and rancid, made him pray to God that the dog would die or run away.

When Spotty was run over by a car, Ouma Kulsum blamed Malik. She cursed him with the worst of curses. "You will wake one day with the ears of a pig!"

That day, silent Salma's protective wrath struck Ouma Kulsum like the arse-frying bolt from the sky which the old woman wished on others. Red-tongued flashes of anger lit up Salma's placid face, until Ouma Kulsum was reduced to wailing. She screamed so loudly that people in the township paused in their daytime idling, and agreed, "Ja, she's about to go."

Later, the street where the dog had died was washed clean of blood and bile by one of those afternoon storms which burst forgivingly over the townships on hot summer days. Malik acquired his crooked way of smiling that day, a quiet way of being satisfied. He would remember though, during his most fragile moments, Ouma Kulsum's hissed curse, when Salma was out of hearing and already sinking back into the autistic silence with which she protected herself: "You will bring nothing but unhappiness to those whose lives you touch." She had used the Afrikaans "vat" rather than "raak": Malik would take—and not merely touch—people's lives.

Ouma fled to the exile of her room where she prepared for death, the slow withering away of her mind, its oblique ruminative thoughts, the decay of her skin and the fading of her eyesight. Prayers said five times a day at the appointed hour and muttered repeatedly in between brought numbing solace, even though she no longer believed in the promised "koelie" heaven. It was for men only, it seemed, this celestial romping of naked houris, for indolent patriarchs and boepensoupas who bought their way into paradise through the accumulation of "sawaab" or heaven-day credits, calculated by the number of arse-wipers they had converted to Islam. For poor-white hoere and township darkies this was a better option than Christ's promise of pious poverty on earth followed by more of the same in heaven.

Kulsum recalled Shaik's refusal to participate in the daily ritual of men exchanging in Urdu or Gujarati the mercenary braggarts' greeting, "How much good have you done today?" Their cackled laughter, when Shaik turned his back. "Oh, Shaik's sawaab will be great, all the Muslim seeds he's sown in nacasara woman." She had consoled herself, in her youth, that her life would have been no different had she stayed with her "volk" and married Piet Pompies after a fuck in the veld. Grey men with faltering hearts would still have spent their Sunday mornings searching with prayer-dulled thoughts for the wanton promise swishing about in the folds of a young woman's dress. Better still, a bit of "blou boud", a bit of sex with a black woman—a sin even dominees defied heaven for. Alienation was for Ouma Kulsum too ancient a burden.

Her greatest hurt now, a pain transmitted from nerve-ends of emotions she thought cauterised down to a well of suffering gathering in her chest, was the knowledge that Salaam would not come to comfort her, would not visit her room and seek her out amidst the swirl of incense, the stench of burnt malfa plant and the sting of liniment which she used to ease her stiff muscles. It was Salma, his wife, who came to shut her eyes on the morning of Eid-ul-Fitr and announced, "Ouma is dead." Gentle Salma for once defied her brothers, who said that even someone like Ouma had to have her death honoured, and refused to bar her children from celebrating Eid and the end of Ramadan's fasting and denial.

MALIK AWOKE to the fierce sound of the dry summer wind, a breathless harmattan rattling the windows in their ill-fitting frames. In his memory there lingered the smell of fat burning in an early-morning fire being kindled, the old-fashioned rattle of the poker across an iron grate.

The bird was gone, and so too were Fatgiyah and Rabia. Malik performed the dawn prayer in the bedroom, seated on the floor in the manner allowed to cripples and the incontinent, repeating in his customary undertone the requisite passages from the Koran. Then he praised God, thanked him for life and health, and asked finally for God to bestow upon him the gift of serenity so that he could dispel from his mind the bird's cry—Ha! Ha-de-da!—and the sound of Fatgiyah calling softly to their daughter—"Rabiaaa-Rabiaaa"—in the dark hour before dawn.

Malik felt no sadness or anger at Fatgiyah's departure, even though it would become the

topic of much gossip in their community. A man
such as he deserted by his wife, surely there had
to be profound reasons for her to take such a dramatic step. And they would seek it out, the sor-
didness they believed existed in all such lost loves
and broken marriages, especially ones that had
outwardly seemed so secure. Whatever it was
that had brought them together, youthful love or
transient passion, the ordained need for young
men and women to marry, until even this folly
was smoothed by the tedious wheels of tradition
and habit, it was not right for them to suffer the
misery of silent incompatibility imposed on them
by fate. Thinking now with a clarity that was not
at all humble or coloured by guilt, he acknowledged: Fatgiyah was right to escape from this
cold refuge, this house that had been expanded
until it stretched the logic of its design to breaking-
point. He acknowledged too, as he drank the
currant-sweetened milk (made especially to
welcome men on their return from mosque on
Eid's day) from a jug in the fridge: he was respon-
sible for creating the empty, private spaces into
which they had escaped from each other, the
islands of lonely refuge which had driven them
apart in the end.

The house was quiet in a way Malik was not
accustomed to. He himself had muted its natural
noises, replacing beams in the roof at the first hint
of a creak, and laying carpets so that the passage
of feet was muffled and no part of the floor, weak-

ened by use and the sun, could become a sounding-
board of the house's age. He observed the empty
spaces where Fatgiyah had removed things
she would need, marvelling at her practicality.
Things packed into hardy, unfancy luggage,
clothes that were not pretty—and how Fatgiyah
loved "prettiness" in everything she wore and
made her daughter wear. More out of curiosity,
he went from room to room taking with his eye
an inventory of things missing and things left
behind. Gone was his leather coat and woollen
gloves, left behind the thin and fancy cloaks Fatgiyah wore to weddings, along with chiffon
blouses and lace scarves. Gone too his sturdy
walking-shoes, steel-capped and round-toed. He
smiled at the thought of Fatgiyah wearing them,
long wisps of hair spilling over her ankles.

The linen supply was intact, sheets and curtains and rich mounds of towels, the squirrelled-
away treasure of a proud housewife, neatly
stacked in a tall cupboard. Of course she had
some money, small amounts saved from her
household budget over many years, until there
was enough, he guessed, to get mother and
daughter to Cape Town and, should they find
Fadiel, to set up a small, matriarchal home.
There, Malik thought, will be her only disap-
pointment. Fadiel will not give up his dubious
independence, the poverty of his happiness. He
was like them, the Khans, like his great-grandfather Shaik, his grandfather Salaam and his Un-

cle Omar. He shares their madness, this love of
things that are not of their own kind. Then Malik
saw the sheet, washed and ironed and neatly
folded across the back of a chair. At first he
thought that it was part of the weekly change-of-
linen which Fatgiyah performed like a rite of religious cleansing. But she was too meticulous for
such an oversight, a washed and ironed piece of
linen out of place, an essential sacrament forgotten. Even before Malik touched the spotless
length of quite ordinary cloth, he knew this had
been Omar's death shroud.

This inexplicable act of vengeance on Fatgiyah's part did not bother him at first. There
would always be a wronged party and a guilty
party, the motives of each side exposed to the
squalid measure of public morality. Sides would
be taken, first shots fired, and yes, how unerring Fatgiyah's first volley was. There was no
rationality behind Malik's decision to keep his
brother's shroud locked up in the linen cupboard,
and Fatgiyah had warned him in her quiet way,
"This is not like you, only abracadabra Slamse do
things like this." Rationality had shielded Malik
up to now from the insanity of his male forebears.

He went instinctively to his sanctuary where
he knew another message was to be found. Fatgiyah, obviously, had shut the study windows
after the bird had flown, restoring the room's
dusty peacefulness. There, on the lectern of holy
books, lay a copy of Newman's *Birds of Southern*

Africa. Malik opened to the page where a white envelope had been inserted. "Hadeda Ibis, a common and widespread resident species... when disturbed are extremely noisy." The ugly Hadeda, illustrated alongside its more imposing cousin, the Sacred Ibis. Malik had grown up in a world without trees, in townships where open fields, willows on the banks of diminished streams, dying orchards of wild fruit represented luxuries that denied humans space to put up shanties or build homes. He had never known birds or animals, except as markers for a fond reminiscence about an age of abundance more desired than real. His wisdom of the world had been born in darkened alley-ways, in swollen streets growing outwards from the city like varicose veins in the legs of a heavy woman.

Fatgiyah too had grown up in the city. She would not know the familial tragedy of divergent species of bird, how the ugly Hadeda had strayed from the royal path of the Sacred Ibis. This was Ouma Kulsum's embittered knowledge, her sentimental sorrowing for a childhood that had had few moments of innocence, birds striding regally in a vlei, their down gilded by the afternoon sun. Before night came and the child returned to the carnal darkness of an impoverished home, life groped at her heart with the twisted hands of an incestuous father.

The note in the envelope said simply, "Eid mubarak, dear husband."

MALIK HAD regained his fragrant breath when Ouma Kulsum retreated to her room to die her solitary death. He knew, however, that the aroma he exhaled into the air was as much a curse as a gift, that the changing texture of its sweetness, warm cinnamon, bitter-sweet grapefruit, the sharpness of oranges-in-the-morning, reflected the changes of tide in his being. There was inside of him a slow metamorphosis searching for its shape. One day it would overcome him, its growth forewarned by subtle signals, the cloying sweetness of decay or a tiredness of faded jasmine. Knowing the manner of his decline and death would not help to stop their inescapable passing. How Omar must have suffered the certainty of his fate, the degeneration from thinking human into vegetative skeleton, a process he was aware of but could not describe, except that it was remorseless, and irreversible from the day it began. Yet this foreknowledge of death was a trial Malik was willing to suffer. There was for him nothing worse than living, and dying, in ignorance. Salaam, his father, had recognised his own ineluctable moment of death and helped it on its way by stepping into the path of a speeding ambulance. Only Malik, and perhaps Omar, would not regard this as an act of suicide, even when it was discovered that Salaam had been dying slowly, cancer eating away at the marrow of his bones.

Malik's conviction grew that the events of the past few days had some grand design, that everyone was a knowing part of its unfolding, even Amina Mandelstam. Or perhaps especially her. Omar's death, Malik being summoned by the police to claim the body, the shroud that he had removed from Omar's house, the funeral and Amina's unexpected arrival at Malik's home, like that of the bird. And Fatgiyah. What miracle whirr of chance had given Fatgiyah the kismet of freedom, an escape from a life of self-reservation and self-preservation, her unhappiness dissolving eventually into a kind of resignation, content if not happy?

He went over and over these events, in his mind at first, then took to recording his thoughts in one of Rabia's English exercise books, after ripping out the pages that contained passionate little essays on Shakespeare and family life in the townships. Her tight, neatly ordered handwriting roused in him a rage of sadness and anger, turbulent emotions he could ill-afford at a time when he was preparing for mortal battle. He examined each event, reordering the sequence of events in various configurations to test the validity of his deductions, the cause and effect of each happening, trying to understand this sudden collapse of his rational world.

So absorbed was he in the weighing up of his new and frightening insights, that he no longer went out, missed Legislature sittings, did not answer his telephone. In fact, he hardly ever moved from his meditation room, so that when members of his Party came to his house they found a dishevelled Malik stumbling like an old man on bent limbs to answer their persistent ringing of the doorbell. Malik was granted leave of absence from his duties. He listened as they departed, wanting to ensure that they shut the gate which offered the kind of symbolic protection respected by evil spirits and township thieves. He overheard without any real dismay a familiar voice betray the secret legends of his family.

"We have to find a back-up. In case he cracks completely."

"Yes, it runs in his family. You know, his grandfather put a gun in his mouth, pulled the fucken trigger, just because he wanted to know what death was like."

This last speaker, a young councillor named Nazier, Malik's second cousin, would prosper and one day be powerful enough to take seriously the question of honour in family matters.

Malik was left with the melancholy silence of his house, and many unanswered questions. Imam Ismail was no help. He had not taken sides; worse, he was neutral and aloof. Somehow his advice to Malik, uttered without the passion of faith—"Pray and search inside yourself for answers, Allah will help you"—lost its compelling wisdom. Even Imam Ismail's once devoutly open countenance appeared overcast by shadows falling from his heavily browed eyes.

Malik remembered that in the years and hours before they died, his grandfather Shaik and his father Salaam had become so loud and raucous in nature that good people around them said Iblis had inhabited their souls and was preparing them for death and eternal penance in hell. Yet they seemed so happy, as if freed of all the burdens of life. Shaik used to walk the streets of the township flinging money into the air. Snaking columns of children followed him about, chanting, "Shake-the-boodle-Shaik," until parents, fearing that he had bewitched their young and was going to murder them and sell their bodies for muti, had him arrested. Upon his release Shaik lectured people about the dark powers of superstition and how everyone was master of his or her own destiny. He put a gun in his mouth to demonstrate. For many years people spoke about the muffled shot, how Shake-the-boodle-Shaik shook for a moment as if warding off evil, then fell into a heap. His brains, it was said, in the exaggerated manner the township loved, splattered the face of an orphan boy, who was destined to become a mad tie-tie like Shaik himself.

Perhaps second cousin Nazier, despite his deep envy of Malik's family, was right, there was a

madness in Malik's heritage, an urge to seek
abrupt and unique forms of death. Life interrupted with such brutal deceit had no chance but
to reincarnate itself. The mystery of our eternal
line. Malik had to guard against those inexplicable, euphoric urges. He remembered the day he
told his mother he wanted to fly.

"I can fly. I know how birds do it."

A countryside excursion, the family on a rare
outing without attendant uncles and aunts—only
Ouma Kulsum an intense, extraneous presence,
how she loved "the open", the pure air, the clean
mountains—walking up the steep gradient of a
Drakensberg mountain path towards a summit
called Giant's Castle where bright sunlight fought
swashbuckling battles with squadrons of dark
cloud. Malik pointed to a huge bird, black, silent,
sailing on its extended wings, its yellow eyes
almost visible, and said, "I know how that bird
does it." Salma ran back to her son. Left behind
by the party of hasty urban walkers, he stood at
the edge of a cliff, his arms stretched out over a
valley of rocky terraces below. She picked him up
with a quick maternal swoop and demanded they
go back. On the hillside across the valley cattle
grazed, wandering along treacherous slopes with
lumbering agility, bells swinging from their necks
. . . a distant, diminutive churchbell tolling . . .
Their heavy tankle-tankle-tankle caught in
Salam's throat and made her panic. She sank to
the ground in terror, ravine and mountain sway-

ing all around her, the infidel sound of Christian churchbells ringing heavily, Christ festooned upon a wooden cross so sturdy you could hang the whole world upon it. She clutched Malik to her, smothering him in her breasts, filling his ears with the wild thump-thump of her heart. Malik's cry brought Salaam scrambling down the steep path, the indignity of dust and loose stones underfoot causing him to prise the child away from his wife with uncharacteristic force.

"For God's sake Salma!"

Ouma Kulsum, as usual, was angry. "Salaam's gone to such trouble to arrange this holiday."

Non-whites weren't allowed in these resorts, he'd used a contact, a member of parliament, he'd paid someone to get a cottage along the river, such a waste.

No one held Salam to their breasts to comfort her. Thump, thump, thump.

"As-salaam-wa-aleikum, Muslim mense, sa-laam, dis labarang," Malbut Amin, the herald, went banging on doors to announce that it was Eid-ul-Adha. The young moon was sighted briefly last night, riding among the clouds, at-tested to by a pious man and his pious friend. Two months and nine days since Eid-ul-Fitr, when Fatgiyah left. Malik peered through the window. The sun broke through the clouds, a day born in blood. One hundred days since the twenty-seventh night of Ramadan, when the dead were allowed out from their captive Janat for a single, precious, mortal night.

WHEN MALIK CALLED Amina Mandelstam she asked what the nature of his intended visit was, did he want to see her in a professional capacity, she as a psychologist or he as a law-maker? Her mocking, coquette's use of this formal language—*his* tone, *his* self-important pauses—surprised him.

"What," he asked, "is your profession?"

Her laugh too, gentle in its ridicule, but so certain. He could not picture this voice belonging to the nervous, fumbling woman he still imagined Amina to be.

"Witch."

"Well, perhaps I am in need of one." Malik tasted on his breath the quickness of camphor.

"Come for dinner then, it's the next best thing to having your ears turned backwards."

He left the house for the first time in many days, the unfurtive squeal of tyres drawing everyone's attention.

"He's crazy. Completely befok!"

"Ja, that's what happens when you drive your wife and children away!"

Malik followed Amina's directions, so precise that he thought she must have mapped it out beforehand in anticipation of his call, deep into the heart of the world his brother had died in.

Streets turned to avenues and the sky was
obscured by the humpbacked menace of ageing
trees. The driveway leading to the house came to
an abrupt halt before a huge palm tree, just as
Amina said it would. Two cars beneath a carport,
one of them the car Amina had used when she visited him in Newclare, the other an old Mercedes
Benz fitted with a special lifting device. A paraplegic, an invalid mother-in-law?

A huge dog rose from the green shadows of an
expansive lawn, walked towards Malik and sat in
sphinxlike observation in front of the car.

"Ya Allah, why do I always get myself into
things like this? To be pawed at or slobbered on
or bitten by this beast. Why couldn't the Mandel-
stams have a high wall and a buzzer like other
white people?"

He would wait. A servant, or a nosy Jewish
mother unnerved by an unkempt Muslim sitting
for no apparent reason in a parked car outside
their house, would either call the police or come
to rescue him from the freezing darkness in which
he was marooned. Somehow he felt that there
was no turning back, though there was still time
to reverse the car crookedly down the steep driveway and race back to the safety of his township
home.

The front door opened and Amina appeared in
its merciful frame of light. She called the dog over
to her, then smiled and waved to Malik. The animal walked with sleek strides to lay his head

against his mistress's leg. A rare blue Great Dane, she told him, bred chiefly for its beauty. Useless as a guard dog. But its menacing appearance was protection enough, frightened people off. "As long as no one challenges it, of course." He agreed with her about the effectiveness of symbolic barriers. His was a gate, a common and sensible township gate. "If it's too high then people think you really have wealth to hide. Township thieves think like that."

"Township, township, township! You people make too much of your townshipness. At heart people are all alike."

His mood became combative.

"Well, there are differences. Take his hound, for instance. It wouldn't survive for a day in the townships!"

Amina smoothed the dog's bristling mane, which seemed so unnatural for a Great Dane.

"This dog is useless, but beautiful. I like it that way!"

Malik realised that he was being teased. In any case, he was glad that he did not have to "test the dog's ferocity". This dog was not as full of shit as many other dogs he had encountered in his lifetime, but still, he would have to tell Amina Mandelstam some day that he hated dogs. He also realised that she was making small talk to cover her own nervousness. She was dressed in a pale-blue Punjabi suit, had brushed back her long, dark hair, allowing her exposed neck to release the faint smell of musk. Not really her kind of perfume, he thought. How Slams she was. Like his mother, and her mother. The art of denied seduction. Suddenly he felt ashamed of his own unshaven, hollow-eyed appearance, the way in which the djellaba distorted the shape of his body.

As she ushered him into the house, he straightened his stooped image, caught painfully in the gilt-framed hallway mirror. He must, he knew, reist the presumption that Amina's chaste beauty was the result of a carefully prepared stratagem to torture him. There was in her a freedom, a waywardness even, that had no need to flout the conventions of her birth. Yes, her manner still betrayed that Thursday-night warmth of women awaiting the return of their men, fathers, brothers, suitors, from mosque. But she had stripped away from her being the passive expectation of imparted joy that men brought home from masjid, the hushed legends of angels and ancestors allowed abroad from heaven for one holy night. Hers was an emaciated wisdom, as precise as the beauty of her body; nothing would come home even on holy nights that she had not smelled before in the clothes of men or divined in their rheumy eyes.

She brought him sparkling water in a goblet, and sat down beside him on a settee, the languid dog settling at her feet. Yellow light glowed in pools around low-set lamps, there were no bright lights overhead. So overcome was Malik by the genteel atmosphere that he sat with tense, hunched shoulders and tried to hide his scuffed shoes beneath the ornate tassels of the settee.

Out of the distance came the squeak-squeak of rubber wheels.

Malik had visited enough of his constituents in hospitals and old-age homes to recognise the squeal of a wheelchair being propelled across a polished floor. He noticed for the first time that the house had no doors, that rooms opened into each other through portals and arches, space wrenched from the body of a once conventional structure. Amina's eyes darted towards the sound, the muscles in her neck tensed. With her rather thin hands she smoothed the bristling hair on the dog's neck until it shut its eyes and went back to sleep. As Amina leaned forward, she brought close to Malik's face the fragrant prize of her hair. The wheelchair's squeak-squeak stopped abruptly.

The torment of a youthful dream passed through his memory, moonlight on the black waves of a river. He exhaled a long-held breath, the carnal smell of a magnolia tree flowering in the early evening. Ouma Kulsum's ancient naked-ness in its shadowed foliage. Then Amina stood before him, straightening the folds of her Punjabi.

"Come, let's eat."

They left the dog in its ornamental pose on the carpet and sat down at a table in an alcove. Johannesburg glittered against the sky, a wicked moonless night in between.

"That's the Zoo down there, the Zoo Lake beyond," Amina said as she served food from beaten-metal pots that required much sweaty art in the regulation of heat and timing. Vegetable soup and an old-fashioned swartzuur Malay curry, black with tamarind, the making of which consumed their conversation for a while. They drank water, like wine, from tall glasses. Malik felt the hard knot in his mind unravel, until a mellowness overtook him. A man inexplicably willing to relinquish protective habits built up over many years, he submitted to the gracious slipping of his cares from their leash.

Until Amina leaned back in her seat and said, "I guess you wanted to speak about your brother?"

The enchantment of glass raised to lip, her tongue drawing her breath from the spice of her own food, disappeared. Her beauty in that flung-back pose became beaklike and thrust out. The unexpected somnolence of Malik's senses was nudged by a sharp need to be alert. He heard the Hededa's scream in the dimness of his mind, but was too tired to respond.

No, Malik answered, or shook his head. He would not remember afterwards the reason for his unwillingness to speak, except that he felt an unwelcome, unholy encroachment, a stir of dust flung against the window. The dog raised its head, Amina drew the curtains and offered him tea. The liquid's heat would bring the food's spice to life on his tongue. But not even this anticipation of the meal's exotic consumption could help Malik resist the utter weariness which overcame him. Like a man drunk from his first taste of wine, he was led to a room where a bed had hastily been prepared. Water poured ponderously into a bath somewhere nearby. He undressed and crept into the coolness of the linen, without bathing, and slept the pure sleep of a child. In the middle of the night he awoke shivering from the cold, put on the pyjamas he saw folded on a chair close to the bed.

The next morning there was a smell of musk on his skin. He recalled fragments of a dream in which Amina removed her weeping face from its rest in the crook of his arm. He looked around him. A guest-room through which guests very seldom passed. The musty sweetness of dust on the bedside table, the ready-to-hang curtains, the glass of framed mountain scenes. A room in which unwanted magazines were dumped— medical association bulletins, *House & Leisure*, *Time* magazines with covers which bore the equally fervent eye-gleams of ayatollahs and American presidents.

If she had been here it was with the lightness of a shadow, and she had slept alongside him with the same stillness as he. He got out of bed feeling refreshed, ready to resume his life. In the adjoining bathroom the water had gone cold, unsoiled, in a bath made ready for two. Two towels, large and small, two gowns, one white, one striped.

Malik washed his face and left the house, taking with him Amina's note which said, in a large and sprawling script: "You were exhausted, drunk I would have thought, except that we had no alcohol to drink. I hope you slept well—I have to leave for work. See you soon?" The note ended with a cryptic capital L and Amina's signature.

He drove home and prepared breakfast, eating as the eggs fried and the bread toasted, ravenously hungry for the first time in many months. He called the Party office to inform them he would be back "in office" tomorrow. Pottered about the house, opened the windows to freshen the stale air, then lay down on his bed, compelled by the stirring of an unborn dream to sink into a restless sleep.

The taste of Amina in his mouth, not sexually, not the protuberance of her tongue, but a sense of its touch, and the salt of her tears. She wept quietly, her face hidden from his. She neither shuddered nor snivelled, which is how he remembered women weeping. Tears flowed down her cheeks with the freedom of someone used to weeping in the solitude of darkened rooms.

She fell quiet, as if asleep, then joked about the portliness of Muslim men. Though he was not as "chubby" as she'd thought. The touch of her hand on his belly belied the childish innocence in her use of words. The djellaba hid his township beauty. If there was to be any future in this affair, he would have to stop dressing like a woman. Yes, she still liked a good old-fashioned township fuck.

This word disturbed the serenity of his surrender. He tried, with a practised swift swoop of his arms, to turn her onto her back, to detach his body from the consciousness of its lust, to take his pleasure fiercely, but aloof, as he had done with Fatgiyah, as Salah-Eh-Din's conquering warriors had with Assyrian and Spanish and Indian women, inseminating in their wombs and hearts the seeds of an ascetic race . . .

"No, I cannot stand lunging men!"

He was to lie still, not move or respond until response was instilled into the rhythm of their bodies. That was her one condition. She would leave if he grasped at her in his premature lust. Slowly, Amina healed the ruptured passion, restoring with gentle caresses the expectation of pleasure.

He awoke to loud noises in the street, dogs barking, people shouting. A fight. She was right, township people make too much of their townshipness. He retrieved Amina's card from the drawer in his desk, where the cards of all the won't-bother-to-contact people had been discarded. Her voice, brusque, on an answering machine. She was working, she couldn't answer calls in the middle of a counselling session, he rationalised. Drawn to his sanctuary, he walked through the study running his hands over the spines of holy books, feeling the hardness of their judgement against his skin. He prayed at magrieb, asking God for forgiveness and understanding. Malik was beyond serenity, even that divinely endowed peace that came with confession.

What had he to confess to? he asked in despair.

Wanting another man's wife, betraying his own? How trite those sins were, the mortal flaw of exchangeable flesh. Malik was afraid of his freedom from the fear of sin, that onerous, elating emptiness with which he awoke. At 7:30 he could no longer contain his anxiety. He rummaged desperately through Fatgiyah's medicine drawer, throwing aside the debris of a lifetime of real and imagined illnesses, vials filled with natural herbs, headache powders and capsules, potent painkillers for her menstruation—you will never understand, you are not a woman, you have no menstruation to cleanse you, he could not remember when she'd said that to him—until he found the Valium tablets he knew she'd been prescribed. Depression, sleeplessness.

"Something to make me forget about Fadiel, my son . . ."

Two Valiums. He would calm down soon.

When the phone rang, at last, it was Amina's voice that was filled with anxiety. "Meet me in an hour. No, not home. At the Zoo Lake, by the boat-house."

The moon, still young, on the dull, motionless water. He had been coming here for years. When other parks were forbidden, were for Whites Only, they had walked around this lake like pilgrims around a shrine. Fatgiyah used to walk beside him, her arm linked through his, the formality of a courtship well-advanced. He recalled his mother's unspoken disapproval when he announced his engagement to Fatgiyah. "Lang lantern, weinig lig," he overheard her saying to someone on the phone.

He shivered from the cold and pulled his overcoat close. The anxious, resolute expression on his face told passers-by that he suffered that demonic affliction, an errant love. They had seen so many similar cases while walking their dogs. Faces buried in despair transformed to joy as familiar footsteps were heard on the asphalt, then crumbled back to hopelessness as yet another accursed dog-stroller emerged from the shadows. "Here-boy! Here-boy!" the cries faded, as lights from the boat-house and the restaurant were switched off in rapid succession. Malik, searching for Amina's voice among those hurrying to their own points of assignation, found his thoughts drifting to the night before.

Her head on his chest, her hand on his belly. Muslim men and their tummies, she'd joked.

"All of them?" he'd asked somewhat petulantly.

"Of course not."

"Have you had other . . . ?"

She remained silent, aware of the potential for trespassed privacies.

He abruptly changed the subject. "Who was in the wheelchair?"

She removed her hand from the folds of his pyjamas and lay back, staring at the ornate ceiling. Faces with ghoulish eyes, flowers forming exquisite vaginas, depending upon the vantage point and the viewer's imagination.

"My husband, Arthur. Dr Arthur Mandelstam. Engineer. Would have made a wonderful Christ. Knows how to turn brine from the sea into water to drink. No, he was not always crippled. Paraplegic actually. The most powerful arms you can find. A car bomb. Israeli militants, Hamas, who knows? Somebody who didn't want the desert to bloom, that's the cliché, no?"

Malik had turned to her in his lumbering, trying-to-be-gentle manner, awkward in his efforts to comfort her.

"He lives with me because he has no choice, we have no choice."

Then she changed the subject, firm but not abrupt. He made a mental note. Frontiers were being established.

"Your breath," she said, "is intoxicating."

Its sweetness like wine, almost haraam. How many women had loved him only for his breath? In the old days, they would have been stoned to death.

Her breasts were like fruit.

"They are tits," she said, "tette in Afrikaans. Your mother had them as well, didn't she?"

Then she was gone. Inexplicably, she had been irritated by his description of her breasts, such a conventional, inoffensive observation, made sleepily, happily. As she stood away he saw a youthful body, nervous and muscular. Light fell upon her shoulders . . . a car parked by a river, his Ouma Kulsum, younger than he remembered her, naked, moonlight on the river . . .

In the car park an engine starts, headlights break protocol and sweep the darkness, figures shift awkwardly, huddle closer. Young voices laugh the laughter of mockery. Malik veers between rage and hopelessness. Suddenly his past is gone, already there is nowhere he can return to without discomfort, without a sense of not belonging. Everything is transformed into the present tense. He hurries towards his car, his djellaba flies in the wind, a white flag of despair. Espying him from the smug warmth of surrounding mansions, residents of Parkside will add him to their legends of the lake. A prophet in drag, stood up by his lover. Wise woman. Or man.

In Newclare, no longer home, he takes two more Valiums. The house does not resist the creeping mist of the blue security light from the street, an alien chill creeps in under the door. Malik sleeps a drugged sleep, vaguely aware that

there are rats in the roof, that their scurrying is
bold. Dreams die in his head, as anguished as
lovers or brothers, are buried in white shrouds,
death-carts with unoiled wheels carry them to
their pagan graves. Persistant hammering on the
door brings him stumbling from his bed. Who is
dead now, who's given birth, what have their
woes to do with me?

Amina is there, her slant of light. The sun is
high. Her eyes show the dark rings of an anxious,
sleepless night. She shuts the door, embraces
him.

"I am sorry."

She steps away, observes him softening, comes
close to him and rests her head on his shoulder,
her arms hang at her sides. All night, she tells
him, Arthur was ill. A conjured illness, violent
retching, burning fever, hollow eyes, all the
things that people die of, the signs that death is
imminent. Made it impossible for her to leave. He
knows, or thinks he knows.

Malik forgives, suddenly understands, discards his resolute anger, his vow to forget her,
fearing that theirs was only a transient encounter,
most of it imagined or dreamed. He says there
is nothing to forgive. They embrace, kiss each
other's musty mouths, make love, fall asleep.
Leap out of bed and moan with mock shame when
they realise it is too late to go about their business.

They eat voraciously, both remembering at
the same time that this repast is made possible by

133

Fatgiyah's foresight. Bread in the freezer, eggs in the fridge. They look at the food, she wonders in her already familiar mischievous manner why it doesn't taste old and stale, they laugh and eat more greedily. They learn the ruthlessness of love. And sleep until the next day when it is time to bathe and go to their offices, making excuses, learning how to lie with ease.

They rent a flat jointly, on the periphery of the city, midway between his township work and her rooms in a suburb which he calls the Northern Hemisphere. Malik divides his life, neatly. Between the poverty of his constituents and the somewhat austere comfort of a love-nest fashioned mostly by Amina. It contains a bed, carpets, a device to play music, cupboards to hold food, a fridge for her wine (always white and chilled) and his fruit juices. He champions the cause of "his people" with less passion but with greater understanding; cradles dying children in his arms—and not just for the media; talks without fearful agitation to young men whose slim beauty is enhanced by the deadliness of their own despair, the guns they carry; chides priests of all sorts for the judgements they bring with their prayers, tells them to pray for life, not forgiveness after the sin of death.

He dresses differently, still in the traditional Muslim style, but more assiduously, has shaved off his beard and is slimmer. There is a woman in his life, people whisper. There is a secret side to him now, quiet and impenetrable.

And Amina, she counsels distraught young women, lectures at the University, is called on to assist at the general hospital, considers taking a position with some or other government commission, decides not to.

"It will give us so little time."

Sometimes they bring with them the edges of their past, Fatgiyah's letter telling him of their son: "We found Fadiel," the tone is full of recrimination, "we found him just in time." Amina suffers Arthur's ailments, his pallid skin and receding eyes that demand contrition from her, contrition she offers with the greatest honesty, no longer weeping but wincing, until her mind feels the bruises of her heart. She tells Malik that she still loves Arthur, that it amazes her how strong his arms are, all this propelling himself about, she thinks. Adds that she loves Arthur in a peculiar way. Peculiar? Malik says. They argue about the different realities that ambiguous words bring to life. He understands, drinks his water and his exotic mixtures of juices, Amina sips the strange wines that she searches out in small shops which specialise in the unusual. During these excursions his courage fails him, or is it his bravado? No, he will not got into bottle stores.

Not even in search of Chilean wine for his lover.

"You can taste the sun in it," she says.

He smiles and knows that it is in honour of some other love. How wonderful that she could be so sentimental, this woman who comes home with the angst of abused and raped women gathered on her like a hard crust of despair. They make love, and talk now, volubly. Shared thoughts are the aftermath of love, not silence or even the drowsy, murmured avowals of love. Ideas, their contest, their agreement, their sometimes fierce disagreement enable them to fall asleep, separate beings who wake in the night and unite once more in their emotions. They are able to leave each other in the mornings, or endure the days they cannot see each other, secure in the two destinies that intertwine or part according to the dictates of their lives. True destinies cannot be forced into being, they merge like tributaries only at the end, when the life span of their flowing has run its course and they are lost into the sea.

He lives only in the flat now, while Amina goes back to her house in Parkside, calls him to find out if he'll be home, as if she's arranging a date. They take turns at cooking—there is now an easy domesticity about him—he conforming strictly to recipes from cookbooks feverishly peered at, she with the cavalier disregard for prescription that comes from years of practice. These are the most pleasurable nights, long, slow hours of food eaten and love made, in and around their bed.

She interrogates him.

"I don't know much about Indian history, but the name 'Khan' doesn't seem very Gujarati to me."

He knows she has been reading his scrawled history in the child's exercise book she picked up from the desk they share, glancing at him occasionally, squint-eyed when she doesn't wear her glasses, and how the squint turns sloe-shaped as a question forms in her mind and she contemplates whether posing it will make him retreat, his breathing different, slower, more deliberate, as he slips away from her through an emergency exit in his memory.

"It isn't."

"No?"

"My great-grandfather was not a Khan. He came from a village called Kholvad in Gujarat."

She muses over this revelation, climbs out of bed, pours a glass of wine, offers him tea or water or juice. She must not let go of the immediacy of her connection to him. Nor does she touch him, this triggers off a defensiveness, that very obtuse male reaction—she thinks—to the perception that he is being seduced into speaking. Back in bed she continues to keep her distance.

"So?"

"So."

No clocks tick here, only their breathing and the distant sound of traffic.

"My great-grandfather Salim—yes, the mousy pious one—killed a man he thought had insulted his sister. The man was an untouchable, loved Salim's sister and, maybe, she loved him. Well, Salim killed the man. How? Probably from behind, or with the help of a mob, never look your victim in the eye, a perfectly normal thing to do in India in those days, to kill someone from another caste or religion if they dared to approach a sister or a daughter.

"Of course it was unjustifiable. Being right or wrong has nothing to do with it. Look at this country . . . for years it was all right for white men to sleep with black women, about the worst thing that happened was that people would make dirty jokes about hot sex, how they could smell 'blou boud' on each other. But a black man and a white woman? Well, all hell breaks loose."

"Your grandfather used that term?"

"What term?"

"Blou boud."

"Everyone did."

"Everybody?"

"Well, white men . . ."

He pauses, raises himself on his elbows and looks at her. When he falls back it is with an embarrassed grimace, the sour knowledge of his folly. She accepts this silent contrition. There is no need to pursue the question of whether her husband or the other lovers she has had, most of them white, desired her solely for her dark-skinned exoticism, for the experience they could flaunt, the smug sense of conquest, even if they never boasted out loud about what it was like to fuck a black woman, "to taste a bit of spice".

Fact: she, Amina, was the first woman he, Malik, had slept with outside of his marriage. In his youth, before he married, he'd slept only with his own kind. And that demanded a lot more daring than having sex with "other" women. Sleeping with the chaste daughters of Muslim men with whom he bent his head in mosque or with whom he celebrated the nikka of other virgin girls and boys, could not be dismissed as mere experimentation. It was an act so indelible that marriage could not be avoided. In the days of the Prophet such dishonourable conduct led to banishment, even death.

Fact: for Amina, exile was a lonely state of being. You sought comfort where you could find it—she explains despite herself, distant, defensive, as if rationalising someone else's behaviour—in cold cities where the sun was not seen for days on end. Or worse, in the cities of Africa where you could not sleep because of the heat, the moistness of your body, the disturbed sensuality this brings.

She forgets about his history, and hers, about the "taboo" subjects they have painfully explored. A more intriguing question arises in her mind.

"Sleeping with Muslim girls . . . how come you never got caught? None of them fell pregnant?"

Mercifully not. The only way to keep the shame of it all quiet. The biggest price was guilt. He relates a story abut the Imam's daughter—"A classic," he says in a quiet, rueful manner.

Malik was a member of a ratiep group.

"You mean you pushed skewers through your tongue?"

"And cut myself with a sword. That was long ago."

The Imam was their leader, chanting prayers in exact consonance with the drums, keeping their sedated minds within the confines of the pure faith needed to dispel pain, prevent bleeding.

"But you had to have pure thoughts."

Any deviation, even the most momentary lapse of concentration, could lead to injury or death.

"And you had slept with his daughter?"

"Yes."

Malik recalls the experience, its beautiful illicitness. One night during a ratiep exhibition, he caught the Imam's eye—his gaze was constantly passing over the members of the troupe, checking their state of mind—the same lovely eyes as the daughter. Something like Amina's when they make love.

Amina does not allow Malik to digress, this

tangential bit of flattery is a precursor to some other intrusive thought.

"What happened?"

He bled. Whilst pulling the sharp edge of a sabre across his stomach, lightly, it was done with light dancing movements, a thin red line appeared on his skin and blood began to seep through it.

"And then?" Amina leads him on, knowing that this too is a memory he has buried and that its resurrection goes beyond the convention of a "painful memory", that bricks in a carefully constructed wall are being dislodged. Or he's playing a game, a delicious deceit she did not think him capable of.

He continues though, calmly and lucidly.

And then everyone focused on him, their chanting raised to a hoarse shout, the drumbeats fierce, the audience silent. Menstruating women and those who had taken alcohol were asked to leave the hall. And then the exhortations to God for mercy and forgiveness continued, unceasing and breathless, until the bleeding stopped and nothing remained but a delicate scar.

Amina does not express her disbelief, but gently searches his body for the scar. She finds instead a sensuality she did not think men possessed, an invisible rivulet of sense and memory along which she runs the tips of her fingers and makes him writhe.

"All because you fucked the Imam's daughter!"

Amidst unbecoming mirth they find their pleasure. Their secretive, half-suppressed screams recreate the luxurious sensation of youthful sin.

Amina caresses the arch of his body which grows leaner each day, he buries his head, mockingly shy, when she describes the dents in his buttocks as "cute". She asks: "Am I as good as the Imam's daughter?" She embeds in his mind the fusion of dark limbs, of tongues quickly whetting parched lips, her fingers search out his anus, she asks, "This is what she did, that pious little pussy, no?" He descends from a wildness, a savagery almost, exhausted and silent. She observes, and dismisses, his inexplicable resentment. The vagaries of men.

Later, of course, before she turns off the light, she returns to the subject of his name.

"What is your family's real name?"

"I don't know. Probably something or other allegoric, like the Gujarati word for 'big stick', or a term that describes a fugitive or a murderer . . . imagine if my name was Malik Goon or Malik Dacoit."

"What does that mean?"

"Gangster's scum, you know, a thug's lackey."

He is asleep before she can urge on him the need to find out what his family's real name was, people who do not know their names have no anchor, they drift. Then she realises how much like him she sounds, and lies awake unsettled by the changes in her that this, this, *thing*—how inadequate the word "relationship" sounds—with Malik Khan has brought, disturbed at her pleasure in these subtle transformations, at the new awareness of fear, a sense of foreboding inevitable within people who love so late.

I am only in my thirties, she halts herself, then admits, "late thirties" with fresh lament. She turns to Malik. His sleep is sure, his breath fragrant, his face so young—and he is sixteen years older than her!—in the shadows of icy city lights kept at bay by the bulwark of the patterned, armour-plated window.

"We live truly privileged lives, to be warm and safe and loved," Amina says aloud and lies close to Malik, reconciled to her sleeplessness. She does not have his ability to mask the mind with prayer, to whisper, as she knows he does to his God, seeking mercy and forgiveness and the gift of serenity.

He gives her a book to read, a novel by Yashar Kemal called *Memed, My Hawk*.

"Memed, that's Mohammed? Why is it spelled so funnily?"

"Turkish. Maybe it's the translator. What do they know about Islamic culture?"

His face, that wilful clamp of mouth and furrowed forehead, impresses on her the importance of the book to him. She finds Memed's adventures too earnest, his heroism coy, a young man all too aware of his prowess, and how macho this is, all aggression and bravado. Yet the very fact that he has read the book betrays a more sensual Malik, a lover of fiction, an imbiber of conjured images, a man incongruously capable of dreams. She imagines Malik as a brigand, armed and turbaned and wild-eyed in his passion. She introduces this image into their love-making. Fantasy increasingly insinuates itself as they caress one another and exchange daring kisses, the adventures of their bodies grow bolder, the tale of the Imam's daughter and *Memed, My Hawk,* daughter and hawk. Malik and Amina intermingle and intertwine. Until they fall away from each other, seared by the tongues and unbridled touches of the alter egos they offer each other.

Now this aftermath is distant, satiated, each filled with a feeling of otherness. He brings the Imam's daughter gently to rest in his mind while she does not know where to locate the implacable brigand. She knows a hunger that Malik cannot satisfy, no one can—she knows—but she seeks it from him more and more, until his body revolts and lies supine by her side. He flees into lassitude even as her body summons from the lower part of her stomach an aching energy, all sinew and taut muscle, too eager, too bright in the pain of her hovering eyes.

"I am going home to Newclare for a while," he announces one morning as she dresses. She does not look at him, continues to smooth the black veil of her stockings over her legs, the memory of a night of failed love disconsolately fresh. He repeats, "I am going home." Adds, with unnecessary ardour, "To let in some air, listen to the township noises."

"You are so sentimental," she chides.

She leaves for work, aware of him lying in bed, his warm langour, longs to return, to kiss him swiftly and say, "There is so little time, enjoy me while you can . . ." but starts her car in the dank basement of the apartment block, drives off into the city's warm hum of traffic and hurrying human life.

Later he calls to tell her he is sleeping over, despite her warning. She has this foreboding.

"You non-believers cannot feel the future," he answers.

She is comforted by the light-hearted parrying in his voice, it comes with intimacy. Her instincts warn her to harden her heart and strengthen her will, counsel that has seen her through many grave crises.

When he awakes the next morning there is a lightness about him, the insubstantiality of wings, his skin is as smooth as down. In the mirror a beaked face that is Shaik's and Salaam's, that has Omar's twiglike sinews leading down into a thin, flaccid-skinned neck. His breathing is high-pitched and uncertain. But Malik is not distressed.

Even when Amina calls and asks, "Are you all right?"

There is fear in her voice.

"Come home, Malik."

He laughs, and she is not annoyed by his patronising tone. She senses he has slipped away. What was it second cousin Nazier said about the Khans? The comment, recorded in Malik's exercise book, comes back to her: "Boats short of their mooring." Malik slips away into a dark well of night water, without moonlight or even stars to steer by, simply glides away from the harbouring warmth of her love . . . no, he is driven away, she decides bitterly, by the uncontrollable tides of her passion, of her *need* to be passionate. She turns to her next patient and, struggling to maintain her composure, says somewhat coldly, "How are you today, my dear?"

Malik walks along his familiar path at the Zoo Lake. He passes the restaurant, where armed guards protect the entrance and men wearing neckties as bright as flags of liberation talk to each other on two-way radios. Some dignitary enjoying "happy hour" drinks. Or is this Johannesburg displaying its paranoia, waiting for robbers to come marauding across the close-cropped lawns? Pine cones litter the path, snowfalls of jacaranda blossom crackle underfoot.

Malik is calm. In his heart, he has decided long ago, there is no point in being fearful. He remembers the story of Leila and Majnoen. Both a name and a madness. Takdier, fate, the one immutable river of life. It is early summer and pleasant by the lake. Busy with people, loud with the laughter of children. He walks towards the boat-house. Rowers who rent boats by the hour bring them to berth with loud, amateurish clunks, climb precariously onto the wooden dock. All have the same looks of satisfaction. Floating on water recreates the sensation of being in the womb. He sounds like an inexpert Amina. Sits contentedly on a bench. The dusk disappears, darkness comes. The same parade of dogs and doglike owners. Here-boy, here-boy. Are all of them male? he wonders idly.

Lights around the lake are extinguished, lights in the surrounding homes are switched on. The blue glare of television dilutes the black-blue of the night. Everyone watches the news. An excuse to sit down and have a drink. Amina's like that. But denies that this is a "white" trait.

"I am not white," she says angrily. "Look at me." Her nakedness is olive-brown, her face oval because of her sloe eyes.

Malik stretches his arms, looks down at the slim slope of his body. Suddenly angular, almost bony. It pleases him. He hears Amina's voice, he thinks. Is annoyed, unaccountably. He rises, hears the frantic screech of rubber on concrete. Tries to place their conjunction with each other, Amina's voice and the sound of a wheelchair. He stands close to the edge of the path, finds the source of the grating rubber noise: a man is parking his car on a concrete slipway used to deliver boats into the water—the carpark is full. The boaters have all gone home now and the place is quiet. The man walks with an easy, wound-down step towards the restaurant. Then a jingling bunch of keys flies from his twirling finger and he stoops to retrieve it. When he looks up there is fear on his face.

A man with a gun steps into the glaring circle cast by the security lights, which have recently replaced the old Victorian lampposts. An actor making an entrance on stage, stepping into the spotlight with a flourish, the way bad actors do, that exaggerated sweep of hands, that macho thrust of the pelvis which serves only to make the audience uneasy.

"Man with a gun," Malik hums the song to himself.

Malik, Hawk of Heaven, or is it Memed, My Hawk, defender of the innocent? Or is it younger still? The Return of Zorro, or the Copperhead? The moment the screen freezes and a voice says, "Next week . . . will the villain be stopped?" And Omar's voice says, "Ah voetsek, you know the crook will die."

Malik spreads his arms, swoops down, before the laughter invades his mind, makes him heavy, unable to fly. The darkness is absolute.

Their Story

FATGIYAH

I ASKED Rabia to go to the kiosk at the end of the platform to buy the *Argus*. She looked at me with eyes that had grown deeper, blacker than mine. She doesn't have her father's bastard blue eyes, strange, even frightening in such a dark face. That's all you look at, at first, those blue eyes with their black cat's-eye centres. He got them from his Boere grandmother. Fadiel has eyes like that. Anyway, here we were, mother, daughter and son talking with our eyes.

You're trying to get rid of me, Rabia was saying with her eloquent eyes.

No I'm not. I'd like to have a paper to read when we're on the train and it's moving and you

149

don't want to talk, and I have nowhere I can go to get away from you not talking, I was saying.

Oh stop it, the two of you, Fadiel was saying.

I'll go, Marianne said out load.

Fadiel put his arms around her, protective, fatherly. You could see she didn't like this. She let her arms fall and they just hung at her sides. It was his eyes, really, that stopped her from moving.

Don't play Mama's games. She knows how to yank people around.

Rabia ran off, Fadiel removed his arms from around Marianne and folded them in front of him. He stood like his father used to, ready to defend himself. Fadiel knew that both of us, Marianne and I, were resentful. I because he said I "yank" people around. Where does he pick up language like that? Not from her, that much I know. And she was resentful because he was treating her like a child. Or is it like a lady? Means the same thing to him, this son of mine. Like his father and my father, like all the sons of mothers like me. Maybe they need women like this, women who can stare a Khan in the eye and say, I won't accept this! She's waiting until they get home to give him a good skel.

Rabia came back, out of breath. She ran so fast I thought she was going to fall. Girls in kurtas shouldn't run. She climbed straight onto the train and came to stand next to me at the window, almost as if she was afraid we would leave without her. She didn't like Fadiel or Marianne. I'm not sure if she doesn't like Fadiel because of Marianne, or doesn't like Marianne because of Fadiel. Rabia's begun to judge people through other people. M'sha Allah, we know our children have grown up when they start judging people.

He's not my brother, he's a stranger, she'd said soon after we arrived.

When the news of his father's death came, Fadiel went very quiet. Then he told us, Rabia and me, that we had to go straight back, he'd arrange two plane tickets. A man of means all of a sudden. Well, I suppose he did have his job. Steadycam. Meaning he pushed a camera around on wheels, filming adverts, TV. My son the soapie maker. He didn't want us to come and watch. Ashamed of us, I think, our long dresses and scarves. There's enough women with hidden faces in Cape Town, he said once, when we were about to go out. Anyway, I decided that we'd go home by train. Eighteen hours by ourselves. There would be time to think, to plan for the future.

You never know with these white women, how they want to get their hands on even a poor man's things, I told Rabia, who didn't want to spend two days on the train again.

Ma, she's not white, Rabia had whispered, trying not to let Fadiel or Marianne hear.

I didn't know who she was talking about, until she whispered again.

Her name's Amina. Like us.

Yes, her name's like ours, but she's not.

I looked at Marianne the day my brother Hashim phoned to tell us that Malik was dead. She walked out into the little front garden to water the flowers. She did that whenever she felt we wanted to be alone, Fadiel, Rabia and I. So old-fashioned in many ways, never mind her skimpy shorts and a T-shirt that hardly hid her titties. She had hair on her legs, like me, and didn't mind. Even on the beach when people stared the moment she unwrapped the kikoi. It's African, very natural and practical, Fadiel explained huffily to Rabia, who said the kikoi didn't look like a real dress. Anyway, it covered her legs most of the time. Long golden hair curled over her sneakers, a few curls even stuck out of her bikini. Rabia looked away. I couldn't help looking. Marianne was an innocent. Like me. She would have made a beautiful daughter-in-law, with some help and education. Why are we always looking for good daughters-in-law? Because our sons are such shits. Like their fathers.

We heard the whistle. I leaned down to kiss Fadiel, but he brushed my cheeks with his lips. A skuins kiss, just glancing off my skin. Marianne kissed more directly, tobacco on her breath, musk chewing-gum. She even kissed like a man should. Her hug was strong, I still feel its strength. Fadiel shook Rabia's hand as the train moved. Rabia and Marianne smiled at each other.

They will never be sisters.

Soon the sea disappeared, then the mountains and the vineyards, and everything around us was flat. Then this yellow earth that becomes white the deeper we get into the Karoo. I can feel the dust on my face, right through the window, which I keep shut. Desert. Dry. I remember this from school, from the first trip to Cape Town when I was a child.

I can't help thinking that Marianne is good for Fadiel. Even if she brings with her the white woman's curse that his oupa-grootjie Shaik brought down on his family. I know Rabia says that this other woman's name is Amina, that she is Muslim. Well she was, once. It's not so much that she gave up her religion or discarded her family. She gave up these things to be different, a woman with something strange to offer. Marianne is what she is, because . . . because she's Marianne. *She'll* suffer because she's different. This Amina makes other people suffer. I heard that she screwed my husband while her own—a cripple!—sat in his wheelchair, listening to them. I try to imagine them doing it, Amina and Malik. I wonder what kind of noises she makes, this different kind of woman?

My poor Malik, he should have listened to the wisdom of the old people, the women's wisdom. Moenie uit jou klas naai nie, they always said. Don't fuck outside your class. No, Amina's not one of us. Even if she's not white.

RABIA

I pretend to be asleep. These days it's easy to pretend to Mama. I can pretend anything I want to. That I liked Cape Town, the mountain, the way the sea rolled in and out, in and out. I can even pretend with her that it made her happy. The monotony, the boredom of watching waves come in and crash onto the rocks, then go out, and come in, and so on. We watched the sky turn from blue to red to black, until it was time to eat on the stoep, which they call a "veranda", and watch the sea and fall into silence. Marianne would light a cigarette and go onto the patch of grass they call a lawn, and watch the cars go by on Main Road. You could tell she was not watching the sea. Her head went from left to right, sometimes staying in one spot for a while. What does she see, I used to wonder? The veld, I think. She's Afrikaans, comes from some God-forsaken little dorpie in the Free State—the old Transvaal, she always corrected me (same thing as far as I'm concerned). Anyway, she remembered that place on nights like the ones she shared with us; outside was something so big you were scared to go out into it, inside you felt trapped in the small world where people clear the snot in their throats, lean back to relax, lift their bums in a skelm way to fart, everyone pretending to be at peace with themselves. It's the dishes on the table, leftover food, the feeling that the day's over. I saw it in my father and my uncles. How the end of a meal could make people forget their worries.

When Marianne came back inside, all distant and glassy, she usually sat down next to Fadiel, more like throwing herself down, letting her head fall onto his lap. He used to look around to see if we were watching, me especially, then roll his eyes, put down his book, a man embarrassed to be himself. He read a lot. Probably so that he didn't have to speak to us, Mama and me. I used to wonder if they spoke when we were not there? Or did they take the opportunity to fuck?

Yes, Mama would be shocked if she read my mind. I think it out as loud as I can in my mind. Maybe she'll hear my thoughts.

They used to fuck when we went out, even during the day! Marianne screamed at the top of her voice, "Ag Here, ag Here." At first I thought Fadiel was beating her. I soon learned.

Mama stirs, shuts her eyes again. She is thinking what a good daughter-in-law Marianne would have made. Because Fadiel loves her in a way that my father could never have loved my mother, not just fuss and affection, sentimental little kisses, but touching each other, all the time.

When we first arrived, we found them like that. Uncle Hashim and I saw them, Fadiel's head buried between Marianne's legs, which she spread ever so gently, not thrown apart like I imagined a woman's legs have to be when a man's got his whole face right up her samoosa. I rang the doorbell first, then looked in through this long, dirty pane of glass—not only township people turn stoeps into verandas by enclosing them in glass—and saw them like that. Uncle Hashim, who'd come all the way up from Simonstown to meet us at Cape Town station and drive us to Kalk Bay, came to stand beside me.

He shut his eyes like he'd seen the great Iblis itself, then pulled me away from the window. He walked off, quickly greeting Mama and me, saying he couldn't stay. I watched him as he sat there in his rusty old American car, stuck in the traffic. It was Sunday and the road that ran along the sea from Muizenberg to Cape Point, past Marianne and Fadiel's little house in Kalk Bay, was jammed with cars. I knew we wouldn't see him again.

Mama rapped on the door with her knuckles, the nagging way only Mama can. We saw this tall white woman with long golden hair all over her body run naked from the stoep—the veranda I mean—into the house. Fadiel stood up and gawped at us like he was simple. I didn't remember him. He was my brother who had disappeared, his dark hair and gentle eyes taken over by this man with a hard face and hair that seemed not to belong to his head. The weirdest thing was how his eyes seemed to have gotten lighter than I remembered them. The colour of dirty dishwater.

What a situation. Everybody tense. Marianne and Fadiel talked all night. God, what could take so much whispering? Was she giving him the courage to tell us to go? Speaking under her breath, her face away from him: "I have no privacy, your mother doesn't like me, you sister is sly, she listens to us all the time, she watches us, I'm afraid to touch you when she's around."

You'd hear Fadiel turn onto his back slowly and painfully, like an old man. He doesn't answer her questions, but talks as if we made him what he is: "I can't help where I come from, she's going through a difficult time, my father's a real bastard, my sister's young, she hasn't seen much life beyond the townships, she's fascinated by you. It'll only be for a while."

He sounded tired, as if he didn't believe what he was saying, but said it so that Marianne would go to sleep or feel sorry for him and hold him. He was trying to get some comfort out of the whole sorry situation, imagine that. I heard Marianne say, "A good fuck always helps."

Mostly you'd hear her cry, snik-snik, like a child.

I used to lie awake hating myself for being a burden, hating my mother for being my father's cast-off wife, hating my father for everything. You couldn't even lie quietly and think yourself to sleep. The sea was always there, throbbing like a toothache, right outside the room I shared with Mama. At home in Newclare, I could masturbate.

It helped me to sleep. Here I had to lie like a zombie between Mama and the sea. And Mama knew that I was different from the child she thought I was and it hurt that I hid from her the fact of not being a child. Or it hurt because she did not see it for herself earlier on, back in Joburg.

I wanted to get out of Cape Town.

I knew Mama would win Marianne over, would do it at Fadiel's expense. She would take her side in the many little arguments they had, like whose turn it was to wash the dishes, or cook, or take out the rubbish. Then Mama would do it herself, so that Marianne would turn on Fadiel and tell him he should be ashamed of himself, letting his mother do things around the house that he was supposed to do.

But it went further. Mama felt sorry for Marianne. Marianne received letters and cried, spoke into the phone in Afrikaans and was sad and sullen for days. Mama thought that her family in the little boeredorp did not approve of her living with a half-koelie or whatever it is they thought Fadiel was, that they had probably disowned her, the father shouting that his daughter was dead, the mother's heart breaking. "Why does the father always 'kill' the daughter and the mother suffer the broken heart?" Mama asked me. Anyway, Mama consoled Marianne without saying a word, just hugged her.

But it was the hair thing that really brought them together. Mama was in the shower and forgot to lock the door. Marianne walked in and found this woman covered in hair, like herself, the same thick hair flowing down her back and thighs and calves and ending in pools around the ankles. The same bushy curls growing from the crotch. Except that Mama's hair is the kind of black that's actually blue and Marianne's is that blond colour that's actually white.

They embraced. I watched them and felt sick. They seemed to love each other's ugliness. I search my body for hair, pull out by the roots anything that does not belong. Hair's okay on the pubes or the head. Doesn't belong anywhere else. One more thing Mama didn't seem to notice. Marianne's crying on the phone had little to do with her family's anger because she was living with a Slams. There was something else that caused the anguish. She kept saying, "Ma, Pa moet verstaan, almal het hul eie natuur." Everyone has their own nature. I knew what that meant: someone in her family was not being "natural". I heard Marianne asking, the way someone does in a debate, making a statement, not expecting an answer, "So it doesn't bother Papa that I sleep with a coloured? Ja, at least he's a man. Oh Ma, you're being very hard on her." But my Mama has very definite ideas about why other people have problems. They can't be very different from her own. Usually the root of all problems is men. Men who take other women, men who find all kinds of reasons to abandon their wives—God, politics, jobs, making money, you name it. Mama has a whole family of women who were abandoned by their men.

So we stayed on. Until Uncle Hashim called to say Dad was dead. An accident, people said, although the police weren't so sure. This woman Amina whose husband was a cripple Jew had her face in the paper. The cripple Jew was being questioned. But there was no photo of him. I wonder what a cripple Jew looks like? Seems he was at the place where Dad fell, a concrete jetty or something. I still remember Uncle Hashim saying "jitty" in that Cape Town Slamse accent of his. Mama had given me the phone the moment Uncle Hashim began to speak. He could only be calling with bad news. I had to repeat to Mama everything he said. She kept on muttering, "Shame, ag shame," as if we were gossiping about some stranger who had died, not my father, her husband. It was as if Mama was putting herself beyond the reach of the tragedy of Dad's death. It was only when I burst into tears, this pain in my forehead, like bright lights which hurt your eyes, that she hugged me, stroking my hair, the way she used to when I was a small child.

Fadiel grabbed the chance. We, Mama and I, had to go back and see what was happening, who was taking care of the house, make sure that we got something out of Dad's estate. What estate? That house in Newclare? A hovel expanded into a township mansion, all dressed up like a Christ-

mas tree, pink curtains and lace everywhere?
Why didn't Fadiel go? Because there was nothing
in it for him.

Mama didn't want to go either. He abandoned
me, she kept saying.

We left, Mama, I told her. *We* walked out of
Dad's house at some God-forsaken hour. I don't
know how we made it to the station with all our
bags. Mama loves getting on trains. I turned away
before she could start her eye-talk.

He abandoned me long before we left, her eyes
tried to say.

The truth is, she liked the place, not just Cape
Town, but Kalk Bay. I could see it in her face. And
in the way she moved. At first she was afraid. The
skollies, the sailors, the Rastas and their dread-
locks, white hippies who didn't wash their feet—
walai! I'm sure they slept in their clothes and had
their sandals sewed to their feet—she couldn't
tell one from the other. Then she began to take
walks in the evening, me in tow, trying to keep up.
She stopped doing her slipper-walk and really
stepped out, as if her shoes were real shoes for the
first time in her life. Always to the harbour. She
raised her kurta and sat on the harbour wall, feet
dangling out over the wild sea. Come and sit up
here, she would say, her voice loud like a drunk's.
It was her loneliness.

At first I could almost understand the pleasure
she got from sitting up on that wall, the sea going
crazy underneath. It was the freedom. The wind

up your legs, blowing your dress into a balloon. The icy spray on your bare thighs. Like being licked, I thought. That was sick. No one has ever licked her legs, no one ever will. Because of her, no one will lick my legs. I am her prisoner, her shadow.

After a while the spray from the sea became cold and sticky.

I told her I wanted to go home, to see that my father got a decent burial. Muslims bury their dead properly. That got to her. She didn't want to live with the shame of not having buried her husband properly. Even if he had dumped her. Abandon is such a sies word.

FATGIYAH

What goes on in that child's mind? She shuts her eyes, pretends to be asleep. Even when she's asleep you know her mind's working. Her eyes never really close and her mouth moves like she's speaking to herself. She writes things down in an old school book. Not a diary, there's no dates or days, just these wild ideas. Why does she think I won't read what she's written? Maybe the life I lived with Malik makes it seem as if I can't think for myself. She forgets, I finished high school and did two years at teachers' college. Maybe that's why she resents me, because I gave up everything to marry her father. She thinks I'll make her give up any idea she may have about going further. Well, this little holiday is over. Teachers' college . . . no, that's a dead end. University . . . who knows? I only hope she doesn't turn out like Malik's family. She has that look about her, even if it's not in her eyes.

Now I want to tell her about my pain.

Here, look at this, in the *Argus*, right on the front page. Last night a freak wave washed three people off the harbour wall. The same spot where we always sat. Only one of them, a woman, made it back to land. She ran naked into the bar at the Sea Belle, screaming for help.

Oh God, somebody help, they're gone!

Imagine, the sea was so rough it ripped her clothes off. I'm sure all they did was stare at her body, those people who sit there all day drinking. Her husband, or boyfriend, what does it matter, and her mother had drowned. Mothers always end up in the wrong place. But the woman who survived wasn't sobbing because they were dead and their eyes were bulging and they were all swollen with water. She was pulling her hair and weeping because she was the only one left. They searched all night, the newspaper says, but no one was found, not even the bodies. How merciful the sea would have been to take her along as well.

That is Allah's way, I hear Imam Ismail say, for people to stay behind and grieve. And usually it's the damn women. That is why we have to go back to our shame, to a dead husband's empty house, to the people who'll come and tell us how sorry they are, to lawyers who'll tell us what a mess Malik's affairs are in, how we have no money, only an ugly old house haunted by a ghost-bitch.

RABIA

"Mama, are you okay?"

She pushes the *Argus* under my nose: Kalk Bay Tragedy—Two People Drown.

Oh Mama, why do you tighten the chains like this?

AMINA

Stille Starlie's sly eyes picked out the woman's nakedness through the gaps in the ragged evergreen hedge. Sly Sarlie, his hands in his pockets on a hot day, scratching, scratching at his groin. I knew that his eyes had locked onto the curve of her buttocks, and as she turned towards us (ah, the luck that voyeurs have), onto the lush mound of hair and the vagina hidden underneath. He was blind to everything else, to the long hair flying like streamers in the wind, to the nakedness of her face as she stared at the sea.

Sarlie is a voyeur. Or is that too grand a word for him? A simple peeping-Gammatjie whose seedy little eyes, squashed between his eyebrows like bruised grapes, invaded my privacy when we were children together, waiting with . . . *predatory* patience, until it was time for me to bathe in the big zinc tub that Meme set up in the kitchen. God, what words I have learned to use. But they apply to Sarlie. He used to carry in water from the tap outside, pour it into the bucket on the black stove, smile his generous half-brotherly smile, that *predatory* smile. Then he sat in the yard, waiting, sunning himself, until he could hear the lid of the bucket rattling.

He watched from the shadows as Meme directed me in my ablutions: Scrub that skurwe neck. And wash properly between your legs. I was mukallaf, "a young woman", because I'd had my first period already. Twelve years old, I think. I remember the steam from the bath, the heat from the stove, the stench of meat-and-cabbage stewing. And Sarlie's eyes. Heated rooms and men's eyes still fill me with nausea. And I hate cabbage to this day, even the smell.

The traffic started to move and I allowed the car to idle forward, until we were abreast of the woman. She stood, hose-pipe in hand, watering flower-beds in the centre of one of those neat, anally-retentive lawns. Her innocence almost too studied. Now Sarlie had either to turn and stare— declare himself the pervert, peeper, poep-hol— or look away. Sarlie was incapable of redeeming himself: his eyes swivelled in their sockets. I wished that others could see him as I did. But

Meme just continued to look dreamily out of the window at the people strolling by, and Ou Dicky had fallen asleep behind his pious eyelids. To make my bastard brother squirm, I turned and took a long bold look at the woman myself. Then turned back to wound him with the naked evidence of my own desire for her, my hands softly caressing the knob of the gear lever between us. What sweet vengeance for every crude groping touch, for the lip-bitten anger expended in spurning the damp crawl of insect fingers along my thighs beneath the dinner table, the horror of Sarlie's jerked-off sperm on the neat stacks of underwear in my dresser, a violation which would have killed Meme had I told her. But I did not know the right kind of words to use at that age. How do you, at any age, tell your mother that your stepbrother masturbates into your clothes? So I hid the sheer terror I felt as I flung the knickers I had chosen back into the drawer. Even now, I have to examine very piece of underwear, held between the tips of my fingers, before I slip it on.

Arthur never understood, called it obsessive behaviour. None of the others ever noticed, not even Malik.

I glanced once more at the woman behind the wild veils of the hedge, bent by the wind, imagined the salt settling on her skin, licked by the sea's tongue after the sun sank and the tourists had been driven away by the Southeaster whipping cold spray like rain off the ocean. Then I saw the young man beside her. A boy really, in his early twenties, his shadow falling upon her bright nudity, as I imagined it would at night between the glow of a lamp and the quiet offering of her hairy river of legs, a silent night-forest of head flung back, fanny and arse nocturnally opened. I saw Malik's face, only younger, a beautiful nose— its hook slightly flattened—a muscly stomach, not quite flat, the tightened buttocks as he stood on his toes and embraced her. I remembered Malik also had to raise himself to my height. It was like being loved by a young boy.

The woman and the boy went inside through a door we could not see, for they soon appeared on an enclosed veranda, their nakedness now visible only from the waist up. Behind us cars began to hoot. Ou Dicky woke up, startled by the jerking of the car. Is o's daar? he asked, then drifted away into the haze of his insignificant dreams.

Sarlie smiled his half-brotherly smile and straightened his eyes while Meme smoothed her dress, shifting her bum in typical Hajji-queen fashion. Then she leaned back to take in the peace of the warm, lazy sea, as blue as she had promised me it would be.

Maybe it was Arthur's regal old Mercedes that made Meme bold. She hadn't been out for a while, she said. Not in this graceful, unfrantic fashion, she meant, but did not say. She went about by train, burdened by the picnic basket she would have to carry, and by having to guide her deaf

husband and his simple son through the intrica-
cies of buying tickets, boarding trains, searching
for early landmarks—There's the Muizenberg
pavilion! two more stations to go—reading with
fading eyes the faded station markers. She managed to get them off at Simonstown safely one
Sunday each month, and leaving the two of them
with the basket of food on a bench at the navy harbour (non-whites are allowed now, she told me
with astonished pleasure), she hurried to catch a
Kombi-taxi to Ocean View, where her ageing sister Astma lived as unloved as herself.

I shudder to think what the journey home was
like. Meme getting off after the crazy taxi ride,
back from Ocean View to Simonstown is always
worse; it's nearly dark, and she finds Ou Dicky
with koeksister syrup stuck to his fingers, abandoned by Sarlie, whose voracious eyes continue
to undress every woman on the pier. Still filled
with Astma's sadness—can you believe it, a plight
worse than her own?—Meme wipes the old man's
mouth and hands with Wet Ones, hushes his
infantile whinging, then darts about in the clos-
ing darkness, calling out, Sarlie, Sarlie, in Allah's
name waar is jy? Where are you, man? You
mustn't leave your father alone like that.

Where were *you?* his churlish, simpleton's
silence would demand.

A dark journey home, filled with the spectre of
sinister skollies and belligerent drunks. They pull
at her scarf—Hey, what does a motchie look like

behind the curtains? Stiek weg die goud, a sisterly Samaritan advises. And so Meme hides her gold bangles and matching earrings, the sum of an impoverished heritage, between her sweaty breasts. Ou Dicky's head rolls from side to side, while Sarlie has to sheath the soiled dagger of his eyes. Here the women suffer the intrusion of jagse men with little patience.

Hey, jy met die hondoeg, wat kyk jy soe? Jy moet jou suster soe gaan sit en beloer!

Why do you bother? I asked today, for the first time.

He is my husband and your father.

We were about to enter another silent conversation, meaning and nuance imparted through gesture, the shrug of a shoulder, the slant of a half-smile. I hated Malik for doing that, for his unspeaking eloquence. I am a person of science, I say to myself, we articulate what we feel. "Externalise" is the concept we were taught at varsity. My mother bent over her picnic basket, expertly packing fruit and bread and delicacies wrapped in greaseproof paper; this mundane grace was the defence she had built up against life's injustices. My smart words would do nothing but wound.

So I say them to myself.

Meme, you are his second, and secondary wife. A Pakistani man once proposed to me, he wanted to "maru", to marry another woman without giving up the first. It was a covenant, he said, that Muslims could enter into. A social covenant conferred on us by the Holy Prophet, so the modern interpreters of our quite ancient religion say. Far from being a sin, it was an act of generosity, not in the conventional, Western manner. A way of "taking up the slack". There are so many widows and unweddables in the Third World. Well, Meme, I'm glad I was too young to say anything but "fuck off". You were too young in your day to say no. So this old man maru'd you in order to fuck you. His penis fathered me, not him. It could have been any man, any penis, anywhere in the world, any man who believed he had some God-given right into and over your womb. Let's be precise: your cunt. Remember Meme, he brought Simple Sarlie to our house, the abandoned fruit of another such holy covenant. That time the woman threw him and his son out. And he lived, this man you call your husband, with yet another woman and her children in a house up the hill, not caring that she could look down on our two-and-a-half-room house at the back of a house, not caring that she suffered the indignity of seeing him saunter down to us when he wanted to fuck you, to keep his "holy" covenant alive. Well, in the end they also threw him out, his children from the first wife, no longer willing to stand the shame of their mother being the first in a long line of legal concubines. Now he lives in your home because there is nowhere else to go. Ou Dicky's dick has lost its divine power.

These unsaid things smarted in me all day, until I saw the Malik-child. He could have been anyone, the product of a gene pool that is not unique, as intertwined as the history of our coming here, as slaves, as commercial subalterns of the white man's empires, as the fucklings of poor white women pressed into whoredom by impoverished families, nurtured on the sour grief of despoiled purity. Lust brings a different kind of consciousness to the body, a clarity in the groin that the mind could never achieve.

Yes, I wanted that Malik-child, the desire concise, sharp. In the rear-view mirror, a final reflection of them visible above the balustrade of a crumbling balcony. Getting ready for sex. The young Malik-child would pull that drugged mask over his face, and pull her down onto him. They want to feel the breathing weight of a woman on top of them.

Yet I wanted him only in the context of the woman he was with. Shit, it was more physical than that, downright carnal. I wanted him in the shadow of her lips, in the many-handed Ganesh embrace of him and her, her and him, in the sharpness of drawn breath, the taste of her sweat on his tongue in my mouth, some hot afternoon like this, bright and merciless, to have him expire in her, her in me and me in him, not just the smell and taste of armpits or semen or drooling vaginal secretions . . . it had to be like death, the light had to die away, the sea had to heave, a giant vomiting up the creatures it had swallowed . . . so indiscriminate . . . blue-green the bile from its luscious mouth . . .

ANNA

The traffic's at a complete standstill.

"I bet you someone's stopped right in the middle of the road to admire the view," Martin offers.

He's still as officious as ever. Then he remembers why he shouldn't be such a know-it-all, or can't remember why he should be one, and keeps quiet for a merciful moment. We examine, all of us with our embarrassed eyes, the quaint, rundown buildings facing the sea. That's what deep therapy is supposed to do, Helena told me soon after they returned, make you know your place in life. Deep therapy in Toronto. Only my brother Martin could be so conventionally exotic. It hardly seems to have helped. We all knew that this trip was a mistake, that Martin could only be cured of being Martin as long as he was away from the people he had offended and hurt and manipulated. Minutes after we had pulled away from our house, it began, all the old unspoken contests. Martin asking me whether I had ever heard from Oscar's people, that brother of his, the politician. He had come to a bad end, Martin had read somewhere. Andy, dear, solid Andy, gave Martin that pained look which reasonable people use as a weapon and Helena gave him her sideways glance that always seemed to sear into the flesh of his dulled consciousness. Martin not aware he was being Martin.

We settled down, a few days ago, at the back of the ostentatious but rumblingly comfortable Range Rover that Martin has bought, the first of his returning-home gestures. Martin had suggested "a journey". There was something he had to show us. A journey it has proved to be. Through dusty little towns spawned in the arid Karoo, as only the British can *spawn* places. Red-faced, imperial trout struggling against the tide of history. And Martin expressed himself on every bit of that history. Carnarvon was here, Beaufort there, a Tommy general leaving a name behind every shrub just as the Afrikaners left their names in every dried-up river or sloot. Martin bringing home to me his guessed-at wisdom, the memory of him, I have been discovering, as he really was.

I can deal quite calmly now with the fact that my brother Martin was a sister-fucker, and that I was the sister he fucked. I've turned it into an object in my mind, a hard ball to be rolled out of the way and kept in a closet, the way ageing people keep photos and mementoes of sad times. It keeps you alive, in a way. Of course, I can't quite *forgive* him, even if they tell me he could not help himself. I squeeze Andy's hand, smile back at his quick smile. I'm glad that it's you whom I fuck with now, I say in my mind. Not Martin-who-can't-help-himself or Oscar-who-wasn't-Oscar. Honest Andy, straight and transparent. Husband and companion. We made a formidable tennis double.

We pass an old Mercedes with a Gauteng number-plate pulled up onto the pavement, the driver's door flung wide. Front wheels in a bed of flowers. That's what makes the Cape so beàutiful, attention to details: flowers on a traffic island.

"Boy, she was in a hurry," Martin says.

A woman on her knees, retching. She should be taking slow, deep breaths. Remember, Dad told us that's what they were taught in the army? I want to say. He said, take deep slow breaths to prevent yourself from choking on your vomit. But those memories are part of the hard ball I have rolled into some darkened corner. For the life of me, I cannot remember my father's face and the way he moved his mouth to shape those words.

We pass the woman on her knees. Vomit gleams in a bit of blue bile on the grass in front of her. Passers-by look away, and so do the occupants of her car, three people looking at nothing at all, in order not to see their wife or sister or mother vomiting in the street. I have a perverse desire to make Martin stop, to offer the woman some help. Andy wrinkles his nose, leans his head on my shoulder. Di does the same on the other side of me. The traffic snakes around a bend.

"We'll soon be out of here," Martin says.

With a sudden twist of the steering-wheel Martin cuts across the oncoming traffic, and the car swoops up the hill towards Boyes Drive. The screech of brakes, the shrill sound of a hooter dies away. I imagine people shaking their heads, not even bothering to curse. Martin's car has that look of crude daring, an upcountry swagger. Martin passes on his arrogance to everything he touches.

We stop outside Dad's secret house, the place none of us knew about, not even Martin until very recently, never mind the conspiratorial sureness of his manner. Dad's "love-nest". Only the English could call it that. A husband and wife could never have a love-nest. I recall our neighbour, Annemarie Bester, saying bitterly that her husband Wilhelm had set up his mistress in a "poespaleis". Well, this particular cunt-palace was really Lizzie's, Dad's mistress. Elizabeth Marsden, or Miss Liz as he told us to call her when we were young. Neither as distant as Aunt Liz nor as intimate as Liz. That was more Dad's style, short and strategically to the point. Thirty years, twenty at least, of mistressing. Surely she knew, poor old Mum. Yes, poor old Mum, I was inclined to think at first. But perhaps it was poor old Dad. Mum was so formidable. Unfuckable. That's the best way to describe her. So right about everything. She was the only one who really saw that Oscar was not Oscar, smelled his bastard genes, the oily stench of his "coolie" ancestry.

Kashmir, Mother.

Same thing, dearie. A coolie from Kashmir, if you wish.

Dad married her for her money. He was the poor but brilliant descendant of a poor but brilliant family of civil servants—the Scottish always *are* somehow, poor but brilliant. She was the daughter of an Asquill who considered himself noble, having been bred since the days of his Norman forefathers for easy, brutal success, but she found herself bitterly divested of this legacy. A daughter who should have been a son. Dad showed them a thing or two. Took their bridal bribe—here, marry our daughter or no one will—and turned it into a fortune.

The gate to Liz's house opens on well-oiled hinges into a well-kept garden endearingly imperfect in its layout. That would have been Dad's demand. Anything too straight or square would remind him of Mum, the she-devil with the ice-cold cunt he was trying to get away from. He forgot that the same womb had given us entry into the world, Caroline, Martin and me . . . and look at *our* imperfections.

The concept of a house with a courtyard strikes me as too Moorish for Dad, though. Was this the doing of the Miss Liz he paraded before us? Elegant Miss Liz with the bun-of-brown-hair? Dad was full of tricks.

Martin unlocks the second door and steps into an entrance hall filled with bright sunlight. The shadow of his face ignites for a lovely, all too brief moment. He draws our attention to a mosaic of coloured glass in a dome above us. The church cupola effect is also too ancient for Dad's rather blunt mind.

"How does it withstand the rain?" Martin asks. "Must be artificial . . . plastic or perspex." The magic dispelled, Martin is ready to be Martin.

He removes from his jacket pocket—a jacket flung over his shoulder in the old-colonial manner—a document which he peers at.

"Yes, Dad's little harem, would you believe?" he says.

Martin flings the document down on a hallway table, the hypocrisy of his indignation sending eddies of dust into the air. Somehow the agonising is a bit too real. What does Martin know, what has he brought us here to reveal, with the theatrics of a truly wounded Prince of Denmark?

"This is Miss Liz's little nest!" I say bravely.

"Who?"

"Remember her? At Dad's funeral, the tall one, stark black dress, slightly greying hair. Durban accent, but not country-club thick?"

Martin smiles though his fleshy lips, Hamlet's smothered grief. "Liz Marsden was his secretary, nothing but the intermediary."

I retrieve the document from the hallway table, but know it will take hours to read and decipher. In any case, its meaning is before us, large and immovable, Martin's manner suggests.

Martin strides through the house flinging open doors, allowing inadvertent sunlight into the shadows, igniting images on the wall. Dad as a young man in swimming-trunks, Dad older, in a suit, Dad with distant eyes lovingly fixed on a woman. A woman whose hair greys and whose face ages but whose beauty doesn't. A boy stands between them, a honey-coloured, slimmer version of Martin and me, growing from baby to luscious man in photographs ranged like the "stages of man" in a natural history exhibition. He was more like Caroline, I thought. He grew androgynously lovelier in each of the photographs. Someone any man or woman could love with brutal abandon. And always the sea behind them.

Martin wears his serious, pained face, looks around for a corroborating emotional cue, sadness, anger, disgust, laughter, understanding, whatever we can offer to give scent to the hunting dog of his own fickle feelings. Helena wanders off on her own, down corridors that lead away from Martin's puffed-up swathe. Andy hovers, close to me, peering at my face. I know what he is thinking: "This can't be easy for her, my silent wife, so easily hurt, so ready to shrink into the refuge of resisted tears."

Dad had a lifelong mistress, and she was not safe Miss Liz. So what? He had a prick, maybe he was a prick, maybe he had a heart in his chest. I still could not recall his face. He was as distant as my mother. I had no feel for them or where they lived or how they died or what they created, if anything. Now this place, and this woman, who was she, what was she . . . Di, where was Di?

"Where's Di?" I ask.

Helena hurries back, Martin stops dead in his marauding tracks.

"Di, Di?" they chorus, voices edged with guilt.

When they returned from abroad, Diana refused to go back to their cold house away from the lake, asked in her silent manner to stay with Aunt Anna. Allison had run off to England with a plumber's apprentice. Martin and Helena would have no one but each other. Di remained resolute, despite Helena's bitter bitten lip and Martin's downcast eyes.

"Uncle Andy can be my Daddy," Di had said.

We find her in the courtyard, amidst the debris of leaves shed by a dying lemon tree, staring at the fountain. Figures and figurines lean up against a whitewashed wall, hands, torsos, fashioned from muscular stone. A glove abandoned on a bench, stone chisels, hammers, a face-guard like a dead warrior's discarded armour.

"Look, he's got a pee-pee like ours," Di says.

We decided not to stay at Stonehaven on Boyes Drive that night. Andy on his cellular phone— already Martin is raising the competitive stakes— secures a number of rooms in the Victoria & Alfred on the waterfront in the city.

"We can always put it up for sale," I say, more to console myself.

"It's not ours to sell," Martin says with sudden vehemence.

"Look, it is a coincidence," I say, "that she should have been a sculptor with a gift for pissing Davids." Young, erotic Davids. Fashioned in our father's image. The turn of the stone-cold eye, that's what I remembered about Dad.

"For God's sake Anna, get real. She was coloured. We have a half-brother we have to come to terms with!" Martin glances back at us, at Helena's disdain, Andy's solid, square sympathy, the laughter bubbling up in my eyes, the tears of relief. At last, I can remember my father's face.

"There's only one good thing to come out of all this," Martin says in his low, I-am-Martin voice. "Can you imagine what property on Boyes Drive must be worth—especially now that the Nats have won in this province?"

AMINA

We stopped in at Aunty Astma's house in Ocean View. After we'd each kissed her on her cheeks, Meme led me to the bathroom. Despite the weakness in my legs and the sour nausea on my stomach, I refused her help and shut the door behind me. I heard Meme telling Aunty how ill I had become, how Sarlie had driven the car through the traffic to Aunty's house, a miracle, since Sarlie hadn't been behind the wheel of a car for years.

He's not allowed, you know. He gets fits.

They fell silent when Sarlie came in. The jangle of keys between his legs as he sat down. A kettle boiled, the clink of cups and saucers being set out, Meme talking at the top of her voice. Both Ou Dicky and Aunty Astma are deaf, and Sarlie is a simpleton who gets epileptic fits.

I wept for my mother and her folly and how her folly has become mine, passed on like an heirloom from generation to generation. I wept for the child I knew was growing in my womb, for Sarlie and Ou Dicky and Aunty Astma, for the careless way in which the seeds of such dull tragedy are sown. I remembered Malik's suicidal fathers and grandfathers, a grandmother who was said to be a witch and a whore, a brother who turned into a tree, and Malik, dear Malik, who thought he was a hawk and swooped to his death in a parking-lot. Even the hadedas laughed to see such fun.

Aunty Astma's lavender smelled of rot, like an old woman's underwear, but it stopped the sea heaving in my head. She hasn't washed her bath in ages, too old to stoop. A ring of dirt tells the story. When last did her nakedness grace a man's? And what does that matter, in the end? One penis or another, some little man's thick dick or droopy dick, who cares? Fucking fucks us up, women that is. Love desecrates a woman's womb.

What shall I do with this mortal man's mortal child, which sprouts from dumb seed to dumb embryo and will burst into the world with more blood and gore than I care to contemplate, yelling murderously its little bastard triumph at the way it has subverted my body, snatched away from me my physical destiny? No, more, this child will rob me of my freedom. I will no longer be able to choose to be cold or indifferent or weary of the world's lovingness, its demand for love. There will be no other option but to rejoice in the feeble, scrawny being's right to be honoured and loved and nursed and nurtured. When did we conceive this sweet oppression, during which night of exquisite idiocy did we fuck and deliriously hold our bodies still, arched like gymnasts, momentarily freed from the wisdom of our sceptic minds? Did you decide then . . . and how did you know it was then . . . miserable Malik-man, that you had sowed your seed and fulfilled your purpose, that your takdier was done?

Oh, how my pee burns.

MARIANNE

Sadie first brought news of Fadiel's "woman".

She bided her time, waited for the right occasion and a setting from which neither Fadiel nor I could escape. I don't think she did this out of malice, setting up her friends as a captive audience and participants in the telling of a tragedy. She did it more out of a need for drama. The telling of the tragedy becomes tragic itself. I think this need comes from within her, from some sad event already foretold in her mind or in her instincts or wherever it is that the beast, destiny, hides.

What a lot of kak, Terry says. For a fris bevryde boeremeisie, you're full of intellectual shit. Like a real university hack.

Listen, I tell him, Sadie's had some unreal insights.

Insights se moer, he says, she meant to screw up your life and she did just that.

What, she fucked this other woman? Not Fadiel?

That's not the point, he says.

Listen, klonkie, that's exactly the point. If it was she who went granny-grabbing and not my lover Fadiel, this discussion wouldn't have been necessary. Another thing, this Afrikaans thing of yours, you know, every sentence juiced up with your favourite pampoen-spreekwoordjies, it's becoming too much. I'm really dik of it.

Dik, nè?

Dik! I said, dik!

We laugh at this self-evident irony. But I still have serious disagreements with him and these other born-to-be-different Afrikaners; they don't use their language except to apply for jobs or talk to their parents or the dominee when they occasionally run into him. Perhaps they too were taught this language with a precision that hurts, no verb out of line, no inappropriate adjectives, no plurals used to multiply single meanings, and an absolute must—never, never, get your genders mixed up. Anyone who used a "hy" for a "hom" or confused "syne" and "haarne" was given the cold-eyed third degree: it shrivelled you up inside and made you doubt your ancestry. Ja-nee, somewhere in this creature lurks a twisted Hotnot-tongue gene.

So, like a child remembering those hateful piano lessons—this key for that scale, but the tone is all wrong, supple fingers wasted in their rigid passage over inert black and white keys— Terry delights in creating discord and clash in his language, a low-toned Capie English lit up by flashes of Afrikaans donder-en-bliksem.

Why, I ask him, impose your hang-ups on someone else's language?

Meisie, he says, you have one hell of an identity crisis.

I lecture English literature to Afrikaans-speaking coloured students in a university created under apartheid. Maybe that constitutes a crisis for a real Afrikaans meisie, the daughter of a judge. My father would have preferred to have me home in Bloemfontein and Buhrmannsdrif, married to someone like him. But that's another matter. It is what I face now that's real. This cruel problem. How you refuse to jump into the sea to save someone you love from drowning, because you know that his own leaping in there beyond his depth was to get you to follow, that loving was a burden; and crueller still, you realise that this is how it has always been.

Let me get back to Sadie.

It's late November and we've all accomplished some goal or other, or we're waiting for something to happen. There's that air of expectation. The tourist season is about to start. Gapers and gawkers, voyeurs hiding behind dark glasses. That's the problem with repressed societies. We don't see the naked body often enough, we haven't learnt to appreciate its revelation as a whole, so we zero in on the holes, the gateways of legs and bums, and that eternal gate-key, a good pair of tits. Rich and poor, from up North and down South, it's the same army of overweight invaders.

We feel the need to celebrate this last epoch of November freedom, the wind dropping its shield, so bitter this past winter, it's like we're all on the eve of something big, momentous. Well, we have a few reasons to jol. I have handed in my doctoral thesis—Kan jy nou meer, *Dokter* Marianne Viljoen, Terry teases. Would you believe it? Fadiel has completed a long wintry shoot in Hermanus, Gill and Wayne are off to spend a long Christmas in Natal, Pedro and Janet quietly reconciled to staying at home, part of the new start they are making. Love's bitter rift sweetly overcome. For the moment anyway.

You had an itch, and not in your head either, I remind Terry. When we were planning the party, you said, Sorry, I have a trip to make, I'll come back when the Vaalies have gone. Join you in the new year. Then we can all get bulbefok dronk. Your justifications get longer and feebler, I tell him.

Get back to Sadie, he says, his secret between us more of an irritant now. How does Sadie fit into all of this? he asks petulantly.

One night at Backpacker's Bar where Sadie works, I talked about the possibility of having some kind of little party.

Who's having a party? Sadie asked, minding our business.

Fadiel and I, of course.

Sadie asked who's coming and didn't I think that was too many for our little veranda and it would be best if we made it a bring-and-drink scene. Before we knew it, Sadie was organising the whole thing. And she did it very well too, biryani and all.

A real little insypelaar, Terry says.

Shut up, Terry, I tell him. You're supposed to listen to my pain, not mock it. That celebratory night, the sky a dark spendour of stars.

Watse ding?

I ignore his nihilism. But can't remember where I read the phrase. Anyway, we had eaten, had drunk and chit-chatted the early evening away, that's the way to celebrate, leave room for the rest of the night. We sat, sated, yes dikgevreet, Gill and Wayne and Pedro and all the rest of us, waiting for the moon to rise out of the sea. Sadie began to relate "a small bit of skinder", beginning, as usual, with a long but subtle preamble.

Much more peaceful now that the Doekie Brigade has gone, she said, meaning Fadiel's mother and sister with their headscarves. Sadie found it difficult to go straight to the heart of her gossip. She spun things out slowly, the way I suppose a truly good storyteller does.

Do you remember the time Motchie Fats and her daughter sat up on that wall yelling like kids as the sea frolicked under their dresses? she said, digressing from her digression.

A wind came up off the sea, rattled the windows. I always think of them as loose teeth in an old woman's head. We stirred uneasily. Fadiel got up and went into the kitchen. I remembered the story she'd told us about Mike and Jeanine and wanted to tell her to stop.

This is not about Fatgiyah and Rabia, is it?

She smiled without answering. Well, the way Sadie begins her stories, you can sense the dreadfulness that's about to follow. Just think back to the story she told us about Mike and Jeanine. Remember how Sadie started off: Now the other night he was crying—wait I'll tell you who—crying into his beer at the Soldier's Bar, because he found out that his girlfriend was scoring with his best friend when he was away.

Whose girlfriend was being scored? we demanded to know.

The tjanker's of course, the cry-baby's. You know why men cry in bars and women don't? Men do it there so they can say afterwards, "I was drunk," while women—

For shit's sake, Sadie, get to the point, who was crying in the bar and why? one of us had interjected.

Mike. She was so damn casual.

Our Mike?

Yes, our Mike.

So his girlfriend, Jeanine . . . our Jeanine? . . . was scoring with?

With Stanley.

Our Stanley?

Yes, our Stanley.

For fuck's sake, Sadie, Pedro had said.

What? She didn't understand our silence and Pedro's anger.

Sadie, you just, just piss out the lives of people, their private lives, right here in public! Pedro said (or something like that).

A couple of weeks later Mike and Jeanine and Jeanine's mother were swept off the harbour wall down in Kalk Bay by a wave. Jeanine survived. But the bodies of the others were never found.

You know how Fadiel always begins the confrontation with Sadie. That night I knew there was no way we were going to stop it.

For such a young woman you skinder like an old hag, Fadiel said.

Sadie had problems of her own, was going
through some private hell. She'd sometimes stop
dead when a certain kind of man walked into the
bar. Usually an older, greying man, one who'd
kept his good looks and taken on a distinguished
appearance, but who betrayed his perversity in a
smile or the way he looked a woman up and
down. Sadie would freeze right in the middle of
whatever she was doing, until the man moved
away. She was jumpy, always peering at the door,
as if she expected a ghost from her past to walk in.
It must be horrible to live in such constant fear.

No, her real name is Sadia, a Muslim girl who
for some reason hates anything and everybody
Muslim. Goes to ludicrous lengths. That night,
out of the blue, she said she wanted to start up a
petition to have the early-morning call to prayer
from the mosque up the hill stopped. When I said
that I found the sound beautiful, she told me that
fucking a Muslim boy was fucking me up.

She was goading Fadiel.

I suppose we could have averted what followed by starting one of those debates we no
longer seem to have in this country. You know,
the newness of a new government wearing off,
President Mandela so relentlessly marvellous,
old Tutu crying for other people's sins before the
Truth Commission. Boring. Who wanted to get
all stirred up about politics? There were other
things to get really passionate about. Fadiel was

in the kitchen brewing coffee in this old-fashioned "moerpot", someone else was rolling a zol, everyone absently watched the full moon rising slowly out of the sea.

You think that's a sentimental exaggeration? I challenge Terry. How about drinking beer in the veld when the moon goes down. Well, here it rises, there it goes down. You have no imagination!

But what the hell, I did find it beautiful. The voice from the mosque, that peaceful voice, a dreamy old man's voice being carried out across the Bay. Serene, that's the word I was looking for. I said it loudly, for Sadie's sake, for Fadiel's sake, for everyone there and in the world. I was tired of being shut up by all the jadedness around me, by people who saw no beauty in anything, who were smooth and hard and lifeless. Yes, like dildos, fucken dull, unfeeling piele!

Only Sadie reacted, went berserk, absolutely mal. Maybe because she's not a hypocrite.

I didn't know what the shit I was talking about, she said. That old man's voice was a "Bilal's" voice, probably an illegal immigrant from somewhere in Africa, being exploited, forced to clean the mosque and do all the Imam's dirty work. Did we know that the first Bilal was a slave, a black man? Did we know that the Prophet kept slaves? You know nothing about the religion! she hissed. Really, like a snake. And gave Fadiel these sharp looks. He sipped his thick, sweet coffee, looked at her, smiled his condescending smile.

Fadiel agrees with you, Gill said.

This has nothing to do with religion, I said foolishly, not recognising mongoose and snake shaping up, Fadiel and Sadie. The rest of us were spectators.

What then? she asked.

Beauty, Sadie, beauty. It's a beautiful sound, that's all.

Ask him, ask your lover here about his religion.

And Fadiel said, Yes, she's right, the religion is in a mess, a lot of fuck-ups today claiming to be prophets, ayatollahs everywhere. But that doesn't change what Sadie is.

And what's that?

A fucked-up little whore.

Sadie retaliated by mocking Fadiel's mother and sister, in whose company she had scarcely been able to keep the sneer off her face. She called them all kinds of names, doekies and koeksisters and what-have-you, and swore you could smell their fannies underneath all that Terylene they wore from head to toe.

Fadiel was very rapidly placing himself beyond Sadie's anger, the way his mother said his father did, and his father's father did, and a whole line of repressed male ancestors before him did. I resented Sadie though. She was placing Fadiel beyond me as well. We'd worked so hard, saw so little of each other, we needed that night together. Suddenly he was bright, cheerful. Everything was about to be transferred to the surface, consciousness transformed to sense. His skin would feel, his mind would disavow.

He said, If you, sad Sadie, were a man, you too would have been an ayatollah. A doh-die ayatollah.

He smiled at our puzzlement.

A can't-come ayatollah, he explained for the benefit of those of us who didn't come from Joburg or know much about fah-fee. Ayatollah Complainie. You yes and you no, you kak and you kou, without stop.

Sadie crumbled beneath the weight of our unnecessarily loud laughter. When she recovered, her response was bitter, a bile drawn from deep within.

Listen you granny-fucker, have you told your partner here about the granny you're fucking?

Silence. Everyone was tjoepstil.

But that's what Muslim men do, isn't it?

She had succeeded in breaching his defences, touching his distance the way I never could. Not the Muslim men bit, but the granny thing. Those blue eyes went colourless. He walked out. All of the others looked away, at the moon having risen from the sea and sitting up in the sky, a yellow, gloating look on its face. They didn't want to catch my eye, and as I looked from one deceptive face to the other, I knew that they knew that Fadiel was up to something, that the change in him recently was not just moodiness, not just that familiar changeability which absorbed light and laughter from around him and made women in bars say that I was lucky, sexually speaking. It must be like fucking a different young man every night. A chameleon kind of sexiness.

Is it his tongue? they would joke.

And I would shoot back: You should see the other one, hiding my embarrassment behind this risqué hard-chick act. Always a hard act, believe me.

Struck by remorse—yes, she is capable of that—Sadie tried suddenly to be humorous about Fadiel's reaction. But her constant sarcasm about Slamse "boykies" had by now built up a resistance and our friends, Gill, Wayne, Janet, showed by their lack of response that they thought enough was enough.

Pedro, however, was more blunt. It seems to me that you know a lot about Slamse boykies, he said.

What do you mean? Sadie asked.

You're on a crusade against Muslim men. Why?

She's like us, basically, I tell Terry, whose real name is Tertius, a Transvaal Afrikaner like me. The first time we come into the city and our make-believe slickness is stripped away by some clever detribalised Afrikaner klonkie from Westdene, we fumble and fold because we don't understand it's a game. No truth should ever be said nakedly. Dress it up in deceitful jest. Give yourself an out. Always.

Terry's mocking eyes terrify me. It brings back the wound, and the woundedness. He silences my compulsive attempt to defend her, a sister in the shit because of her loud mouth. I'm not confronting the issue, he says finally.

Sadie walked out into the night. Its splendour of distant stars, cold blue eyes in a black face. Ungently led by Pedro, who said that it was my own fault for being so dumb and so blind, my friends told me about Fadiel's piece of skelm, his bit on the side. Like shock therapy. It hurts like hell and is supposed to pass.

She's dark, or darkish, long hair, kind of black, you never see her eyes.

Yes, always wears dark glasses.

And her clothes are strange, very formal, even when she's all got up in her "leisure wear".

Funny to see her walking along Main Road in those swish-swishing dresses.

Silk soutane gowns, naked at the back, right down to the arse. You see lots of them in Singapore, mostly worn by whores.

Yes, exotic, if that's what you think of konfyt.

Rich. Not exactly young.

Only, the pain stayed, and is still there, ruminative, rousing, anger changing to despair, changing to a distancing I fear even more. I sought refuge. Not in eccentricity. I couldn't wear the coils of fortune-beads Gill gave me, the mere thought of their weight was depressing. Or go for polarity therapy or sit cross-legged with Janet on the podium at the fisherman's promenade, reciting mantras to the god of wounded, liberated women. I did take a big risk once, picked up a young sailor in this horribly uptight bar in Simonstown. But he turned out okay, didn't fumble much with the condom I handed him from the depths of my still-fettered passion. It was just the way he kept saying "Jurre" whenever he got caught in the veils of my hair, and the way he ran his hands through its lengths, like I was some sea creature. I fucked a monster from the ocean, and she screamed "Naai me! naai me!" on top of it all! he'll brag to his chommies tomorrow. I threw him out, told him my lover was a coloured gangster and he, little sailor boy, shouldn't return. He grinned as if to say, Ja, tell me another one, and sauntered off along Main Road. A man well-fucked, at peace with his world for the night.

I took refuge in books and music and silence and tears and screams, in too much booze once or twice, in the frenzy of doing mundane things endlessly. You're a bit manic, Janet would say in her accidentally unkind way. Then she stopped coming, just as Gill had stopped, and I only had Terry to talk to. He listened and responded sharply, no bullshitting him, but always caringly. He sat there watching me as I worked in the garden, my little

Eden. I trimmed the lawn and helped the red bougainvillaea climb like a beautiful, scarlet birthmark up the old, gray walls of the house, planted new rose-bushes, nursed the nasturtiums even though Terry said they'd die in this humid weather. Only the hedge I left untouched. This wild, wind-tortured hedge which demarcated my paradise from the world streaming by in their holiday cars. I didn't even mind those prying eyes, staring at my nakedness.

Be careful, Terry warned.

About what, these loer-koekeloer tourists? I would turn and give them a full frontal. You never seen doos before?

No, not them, Terry said, your motives for becoming such an exhibitionist. You know what happens to those alles-op-skou meisies, no?

Then Fadiel came back. One day while I was in the garden, naked, the wind in my hair, salt on my skin, that class of way-out pleasure. Fadiel came up from behind and embraced me. Terry fled. I turned and smelled on Fadiel a grief, like the smell of old fat in the workers' pondokkies on the farm. It marks you with the smell of slavery all your living life. I responded instinctively and put my arms around him. He led me up the stairs and folded me across the bed as if I were some piece of fancy cloth. He bent over, with the sunlight from the window behind him, and cast a dark shadow across my face. He reeked of age and death. My placidness defeated him, my uncaring open-leggedness, this submission that was not a defeat.

There, my little darling, there's some cunt, meaningless flower of flesh. It does not rule my soul. These and many other things I could have said to Fadiel as he slumped down on the bed, sated, shoulders hunched, his penis slowly sinking, a tired flag, another empire at sunset.

These and other things. So, where's your piece of Slams konfyt? Or: do you know what happens to little boys who play with fire? They pee in their beds. Something prosaic, quaintly Afrikaans, because that's what's expected of me? Or was it something quaintly womanish I had to say?

I had nothing to say. I remember rising from the bed without triumph or sorrow. I thought of finding Terry, saving him from his gentle cowardice and saying, Let's go away.

I made a courtesy call to Fadiel's mother. Told her he doesn't look good, perhaps they should send someone to fetch him. Then made the mistake of being wise. With a woman twice his age, old enough to be his mother, it was bound not to work out, I said. A bitter taste in my mouth. I had to watch that. Despair leaches out, rust from an iron rod.

We all have our mapped-out coordinates, those veins of road past familiar landmarks, back to beginnings which appear more significant than they are or even ought to be. You leave the NI north and take a lesser road to Kimberley, and a

lesser road still to Vryburg, and then on to Stella.
Madibogo provides a pleasant little detour, a road
darkened by tall tree-lined wind-breaks planted
by some drunken visionary. The exotic dryness
of the veld turns to dust, slowly, deliberately, so
that the traveller is forced to observe: here the
lives of man begin. This season, though, the rains
have been good. Some weather system out there
which switches its gender, El Niño becomes La
Niña and wreaks havoc with the patterns of
nature we sowers and planters and tamers of the
earth think we can read infallibly. There that's the
boeremeisie talking, we never forget our close-
to-the-earth insider's knowledge.

But this wetness is temporary, it makes the
world look artificial, too *pretty*. We're more accustomed to dust.

Remember, Terry, during the drought that
time in the Free State, when Ma had to cover
everything with cloth—cutlery, cups, plates,
food—or this red powder would contaminate
everything? And we still tasted it, fine, spicy, like
curry-powder almost. These days that "rooigevaar" is more daring, more dramatic. I saw photos of entire fields buried under the stuff, the sun
blotted out . . . and here the hovels begin, the little cities in the veld, aptly named Rooiground . . .
I am almost home.

My memory seduces me. I remember, as you
turn off along the Jagersfontein road towards
Botswana, you're suddenly at number two, a

farm without a name. Small, contained, green. The stoep—never could stand the word veranda, so pretentious—cool and dark at this time of the day.

And what awaits me there? The requisite bitter, withdrawn father. Not because of what I am, but because of what he is. I remember Fadiel's sister Rabia whispering to her mother: I think she's got moffies in her family and it's killing her father and mother. Would that that was the sum of our troubles. God, all this obsession with sexuality. History is a much more distressing burden.

I was a soldier. I did what was expected of me then.

He is like Fadiel and his family. They never say things, they force you to guess, to divine, to smell out the thoughts that bother them, like an abscess in the mouth which they never admit to but which they constantly worry with their tongues, letting loose a sour rot.

Nor do you hear the other voice inside my father say, Some remorse perhaps?

It was a war, damn it, a war, the familiar, patriotic voice thunders. Stony-faced, stoic, he still shaves every morning, lathering with soap. It was his clean, manly smell that made me love him in the beginning, and fear him in the end.

He's expecting a subpoena from the Truth Commission, my mother says. My mother, the requisite suffering woman, thin, worn down with worry about his health and her own, about his ability to manage the farm. This amnesty thing occupies his mind all the time, she tells me. She regrets instinctively that I am not a man, more than she regrets my politics or my sex life. These deviations you can deal with, it is the business of running a business that needs a straightforward, khaki-wearing, quiet-faced man.

He won't just go on his own? I'll try and urge, gently.

No, he has too much honour for that.

A soldier who cries is lost. Like Christ's puritan hosts. Martyrs don't cry.

There it is, a Dutch gable in the veld, father's family home. His father and his father's father began their journeys here. I must conceal Terry from them, hide him deep inside of myself. You'd like to hide in my womb, wouldn't you? Fadiel was right. Perhaps all you ever wanted after all was to get me into bed.

FADIEL

She's gone. So what? She had her little voices. Listen broer, she's got this guy in her head, talks to him, she's even given him a name. Terry. Shit. Tell me about befok. I'm sure, even when we were screwing it was this Terry she was thinking about. If anything's going to mess your life up, it'll be a woman. They never stand by you in the end. They don't understand braskap. Men understand that. Brotherhood. I'm your bra no matter what.

This thing with this other woman? Look, bra, I know I fucked it up with Marianne. But she was something else, this woman I mean. Just like Marianne was something else. Shit, she was so koe'-sister, you noch?

God, I can't even begin to tell you. Like flowers, warm flowers.

She just disappeared one day. No warning. You know what's weird? She left nothing behind. Take Marianne, a few shirts, some panties she left on the line, little things. A presence, a smell. This woman, not a thing. Hey my bra, it was worth it. All the fucken pain. She was a woman, a real woman. Not one of these little goosies with their feathery little dosies.

Nothing to Confess

WHEN AFTER a long time the policeman did not return, Amina Mandelstam stood up and went to the window. She sensed the ferocity of the wind, its invisible curled-tongue licks on the ingrained dirt of the window-pane. The wind blew across the mine-dumps, depositing a fine white silt on buildings and cars, little dervishes danced up the streets in swirling skirts; from here, or from down there at least, the road ran up all the way, along the old main road through Fordsburg, Mayfair, Langlaagte, along the railway line, all the way to Newclare. She could see none of this from the tenth floor of the police building. Here, so Malik told her, he had been detained, a long time ago. After the second week in solitary confinement he had sent his mind on a journey home along that route, and repeated the journey each day at the same time, late afternoon, slowing to a crawl in peak-hour traffic, taking short cuts through back routes his father had used to smuggle contraband past police roadblocks. Until Fatgiyah sensed his presence and prayed and then laughed. Fatgiyah seemed happiest then, having Malik without having to put up with him.

Amina brought her mind back, reeling it in just as Malik must have done. Old John Vorster Square. From here they had flung their political enemies—not necessarily the most dangerous of them—to their death, here they had marched the leaders of the land blindfolded through the dull mystery of long, winding corridors. You counted the number of stumbled paces from your holding cell so that you knew where you were being taken to, prepared yourself for what was to come. Fifteen paces, she supposed, could have been the worst: Colonel Venter's office. Here you prepared yourself for flight, first to be "helicoptered" around by your armpits and then out through the window.

"The detainee jumped," they said afterwards.

Startled by the logicality of her memory, Amina recalled the voice of at least one person she knew who had had "a near thing" on John Vorster's tenth floor. In exile, he recounted with piqued irony the miracle of his release, some quirk in his captors' nature or the inconsistency of their brutal system, he was after all an important "catch" they had let go. Spared a martyrdom that every-

one thought he had reconciled himself to, his
inadvertent life of freedom, was lived resentfully.
He had worn his burden of disillusion with fierce,
schoolboy pride, vindictive in his constantly
wound up political fervour—she and others imagined him cranking up the lever marked patriotism
each morning before breakfast, the way Buddhists
meditate or Jesuits kiss bitter stone floors—and
eagerly participated in witch-hunts, he is a "Work-
erist", she a "Trot", they have "anti-progressive"
tendencies.

Somehow it didn't matter, now. The man, in
parliament or government somewhere, no longer
repeated the story of his escape from death in
breathlessly graphic detail, comedy balancing
pathos ("Colonel Venter said, 'We're going to
serve the beggars curry-moer on the pavement!'"), now that massacres, secret poisonings,
letter-bombings were being confessed to everywhere. Anyway, he was a bad lover. The Ameri-
cans have this wonderful word: lousy.

She recalled other faces, their places in the
hierarchy of remembered things, thin smiles,
crooked teeth, bald heads, Gandhi-like old-angel
scowls. Exiles had created their own insuperable
divisions. There were the strategists—members
of the leadership—who trusted and confided,
others who were trusted and confided in, a few
whose exotic suffering bestowed on them special
status, their names called out at commemorative
events. Then there were those who were not

trusted and quietly shunned. The rest were simply peripheral, the wife or husband or lover of
someone, and like Amina, they often ended up as
the estranged partner of a "figure" in the Move-
ment, allowed to drift along on the social eddies
created by struggle occasions.

"The first duty of an underground organisation is to protect its secrets," a lawyer once told
her, compelled by his patronising sense of honour
to make small talk after a one-night stand. Like
social ants in a hugely stratified colony, the
peripherals were still regarded as part of the
"broad struggle", welcome at parties or into
lonely beds in hidden rooms, solitary people who
loved and were loved with desperate quickness,
transient passions that enabled life to continue.
Amina belonged to these hosts of "reference
points" which members of the liberation move-
ment created for each other in cities around the
world. Not just someone to sleep with, someone
to provide instant release from "struggle pressures", but someone with whom a native familiarity could be shared, a comfortable understanding, a Joburg or Cape Town or Durban
phrase which might reignite the longing for
home. This helped exiles to hope, even if most did
not even half-believe that liberation would come.
Amina was not used and abused, or if she was, it
was a willing participation in a charade of com-
radely promiscuity, herself readily using and
abusing.

Until Arthur. Until she met and fell in love with this "white lefty" who was so passionate about his work that he went to live in Israel to practise it, this craft of divining water in deserts and channelling its bubbling magic along pipes to drip-drip with sacred slowness onto experimental vegetable plots. A Jew going to Israel to grow gigantic tomatoes, what was wrong with that?

They both were.

Remember at University? Arthur was the guy who never took part in demonstrations, but was always urging them on, never handed out a pamphlet, was always on the outside, circling on the ring road of political activism. Enough to make him seem suspect. And then, to go and live in Israel! What about Amina? Oh, a sleeper. Well, she slept around, even, it was rumoured, with President Samora Machel. He was the big name the gossips dared to mention, they were beyond his vengeful reach; there were others equally prominent, in more strategic positions right within the organisation. She'd fuck anything, man, woman, even child, it was said. Remember how she dumped Comrade So-and-So?

How much does she know about the leadership?

What do you think they talk about in bed?

Makes her suspect too, even Mossad gives our people briefings on people like her.

Amina lit a cigarette, impatient now for the

policeman to return. She sat down, slightly dizzy from the deep inhalation of cigarette smoke. She had only recently started smoking again, after nearly ten years. The craving had started, she recalled, the moment she hoisted herself up from the toilet in Aunty Astma's house in Ocean View and brusquely told her mother it was time to go. She had not addressed Ou Dicky or Sarlie or waited to see if they were following as she marched to the car.

The door opened. The passage beyond, cool and dark. The elderly Afrikaans policeman had with him now a younger one full of unsmiling authority. A voor-op-die-wa, Amina thought. The older one remained as bored and uninterested as before. The younger began his "I want to ask the relevant question" routine.

The cigarette tasted bitter against the tip of Amina's tongue. She interrupted him. "There is nothing I can tell you that I didn't already tell your colleague. I have nothing to confess."

He spoke in an Afrikaans-inflected English, his South Africanisms flattened, or was it rounded, like hers, "r's" not quite as slurred, "ch" sound impeccably elongated. How many years in New York or Toronto or London, or Dar es Salaam even? His face half obscured by the simple-minded cubicles boldly marked in, out, refer-in, refer-out, for signature, he told her quite simply that she had no choice, she was "his" in this room.

A slight smile, intended to be ironic, revealed an innate cruelty. He asked the older policeman to leave them alone.

A ruthlessness, at the least, Amina thought.

He wanted to check some facts.

Yes, my name is Amina Mandelstam. Yes, married, or was, to Arthur Mandelstam.

Yes, I am thirty-six years old, a South African citizen. By birth.

My maiden name? You mean my unmarried name, no?

Born 6 February, Strand. In the Cape.

No, I have never renounced my South African citizenship, and I have applied for my South African passport to be restored to me. No, I do not have a criminal record.

We all do? Perhaps you speak for yourself.

Yes. Well, I became acquainted with Mr Khan through his brother, or through his brother's death, to be precise. I treated his brother for depression. He showed signs of schizophrenia, or multi-personality syndrome. Yes, I am medically trained—I specialised in diseases of the nervous system. I practise as a clinical psychologist because I am trained as one as well. And because the Medical Board still will not recognise my medical qualifications. I studied in Cape Town and Cairo. Yes, and Tel Aviv, yes.

His brother? Anxiety and severe paranoia. Got worse when his wife left him. Thought he was degenerating. Returning to vegetable matter. No, it was not a case of a man thinking he was a carrot. I think sir, that this line of questioning is offensive. Perhaps you want to call one of your superiors, who perhaps has a *little* more of an understanding of these matters? Yes, I am talking about the science of the mind.

Good. Let's confine ourselves to the case of Mr Khan, let's do that. Yes, it is true that I went to see Mr Khan after his brother's death. I returned from a trip abroad—Italy—my husband, Dr Mandelstam, was in Venice to see a neurosurgeon we thought might help to restore the use of his legs.

His injury? That's on record. A car bomb in Haifa. Israel. No one claimed responsibility. I thought we agreed to confine . . . good.

I went to see Mr Khan because I was very surprised at his brother's death. He was doing well, was able to talk quite coherently. Before? He was wasting away. Refused to eat, or could not eat, though doctors could find nothing physically wrong with him, except for some peculiar problem with his breathing. They could have addressed the problems through surgery. But Oscar, or Omar, would not give his consent. So, when I returned from Italy I found that he had died. The police suspected no foul play. No, nor do I. It's just that, well, he was buried so quickly. Initially I wanted Mr Khan to consent to having his brother's body exhumed, an autopsy . . . medically speaking, he was a unique case.

No, it became evident that Mr Malik Khan,

Oscar's brother, would never allow that. He was too staunch in his Muslim beliefs. Sir, my religious beliefs are none of your business and irrelevant to this case. If you are going to persist . . . please, make sure you do.

A while after Oscar's death, a month, two, I received a call from Mr Khan. He sounded distraught and asked to see me but refused to come to my rooms. For political reasons I think. A man in his position seeing a psychotherapist. He may have been too embarrassed. So he came to my house.

Yes, we had a relationship.

Yes, he's dead. And his brother. Yes, Arthur too.

My stepfather and stepbrother? A coincidence, of course. I do not control the destinies of individual human beings. What do you mean "How many others?"

What?

I have no idea whether anyone in Israel or Canada or anywhere else, men with whom I have had relationships, are dead . . . do you follow the lives of everyone you've slept with?

And by the way, it's "whom" not "who", Amina wanted to say. Something to put this conversation back into its place, restrict the passage of this Boertjie's monotone voice—a farmer turned guerrilla turned cop, the struggle has its contradictions—to the known facts, to the obvious realities he seemed determined to subvert.

But in the end she closed her eyes, indulgently.
Yes, she thought, indulge him, this little general
who has come back from exile to be a better fas-
cist than them.

MARTIN HAD always hated being alone. As a
boy he was quite content to sit by himself in his
room, examining his coin collection, placing new
acquisitions into their appropriate places, cata-
loguing their history onto index cards, happy—
smug almost—with his precocious success as a
numismatist. Until he became aware that the
noises in the house, footsteps, a tap being opened,
a cistern flushing, were no longer there. Then he
would panic, run from his room, and search the
house for some human presence. Anyone, his
father napping in his study, his uncommunicative
mother pottering about in her famous rose garden,
his two sisters playing their mysterious games, a
servant or a gardener even, would provide enough
reassurance to slow his racing pulse. He had no
need to speak to them; their being there was
enough.

On the rare occasions when Martin found the
house empty he walked agitatedly from room to
room. Driven by an anger he could not compre-
hend, he became destructive, decapitating prize
roses in Grace's garden, disturbing, with the brutality of a policeman going through a suspect's
belongings, Caroline and Anna's neat cupboards.

When the family returned, often from very disparate errands, they would find the house in inexplicable disorder. No one dared to confront Martin, who had by now returned to his room and was busy with his coin collection. He had always managed, in the end, to control his distress, and was able to refute, with no more than s smile, Caroline's accusation: "It must be Martin; there was no one else in the house."

Now Martin was confronted by the same, panicked feeling of being left alone without warning. Helena had gone off somewhere. What bothered him was not the possibility that she was having an affair, for which she would pay the inevitable price of guilt afterwards, but that she had left without his knowing. He had been working in his study, absorbed in analysing stock-market trends—now that he had left the university there was nothing to do but make money—when he realised that the house was empty. He could no longer hear Helena tip-tapping on her computer, the distant rustle of pages as she paused in her writing to refer to her notes. The kitchen too was quiet, Rosina must have gone off as well. How unlike other domestics she was, gliding unobtrusively in and out of the house, never asking for more than was due to her.

Knowing that he was alone was not enough to satisfy Martin's paranoia. He went first to Helena's study to confirm her absence. The lamp glowed warmly on her desk, the screen on her computer, left on, had switched to a pattern of radiating stars. She had certainly left in a hurry, as if summoned urgently. But Martin could not remember hearing the phone ring or anyone at the door.

He looked around the book-lined room. New publications, journals and papers he had not seen arrive, were set out on a table waiting to be read. It struck him that Helena's study had a monastic atmosphere which resisted the modernity of the rest of the house, and that she lived *here*. What happened in their bedroom, or at the dinner table, or in the bathroom which they often used together, was no more than enforced co-habitation.

He went next to the kitchen, which he found in darkness. Perhaps Rosina knew where Helena had rushed off to. But the back door was locked and he could not locate the key. He peered through the window. Rosina's room was in darkness as well. Was this her day off?

Why did he never know these things?

Martin tried to calm his nerves by watching television. He was distracted for a while by an item on the news which dealt with the death of an NIA agent whose throat had been cut by a woman he was interrogating. Martin recalled seeing in the papers the pictures of Malik Khan, and of Oscar, who seemed too young for his face, and of a man called Mandelstam. Apparently they had been murdered by the same woman. Two serious coolies and a smiling Jew. So what?

He turned up the volume until the news-reader's voice filled the house, then resumed his systematic search. In Allison's room he found the familiar mementoes of a privileged childhood. Hand-drawn portraits on paper yellowing with age, discarded old school hats and sports-day rosettes. He had forgotten he had a daughter named Allison. She probably chose not to remember she had a father named Martin. He fought off a new, more precise anguish as he recalled Allison's face. "At least there's nothing to hate in here," he said forgivingly to himself.

Diana's room was not much different. He sat on the bed, which felt lumpy and gave off a smell of dust, strong and spicy, like mustard or cinna-mon left to go old in a cupboard. Not surprising, he thought, considering that it was the one room in the house people seldom entered. He suspected that Rosina often sat or even napped in Allison's room, which was sunny and quiet. But this harmed no one and he had never chastised her for it.

I'm becoming damn soft, he thought. And then: Why do we find Diana's room so forbid-den?

Little angelic Di, who was no longer so little, accompanied Martin on weekly outings—one hour every Saturday—to the mall, where they ate lunch in silence. Di had learned the grown-up art of avoiding painful things. She would never ask, for example, "Tell me Dad, is it true, did you really try to molest me or were you just being affectionate?" Not even when she grew up and became a redoubtable woman like her Aunt Anna. Half an hour after they left Anna's house—on the dot, he had timed it—she would call on the mobile phone with which she had armed Di, to ask, "Are you okay, is Martin being nice?" Anna had insisted on this futile ritual, this way of "keeping in touch". He knew that it was her way of punishing him, forcing him to face his "weakness", and so to keep it in check. He often wondered how many other fathers sitting there, elbows on the table, hands under the chin, were actually child molesters doing penance.

Once he had tried to get Diana to talk about the fact that she lived with her aunt. "Aren't you even in the least interested to know why you are not living with your own parents?"

"Anna and Andy are my parents," Di had responded sternly. "They respect my views. We may disagree, but at least they are willing to listen." Then she looked away. Subject closed.

Martin imagined the dinner-table debates, ideas contested as the salt was passed and the wine poured—one glass won't do her any harm. Everybody on first-name terms. They would ask, "Di, are you sexually active?" or something oblique like that. Talk about safe sex, about taking responsibility. "She'll have to learn to deal with these issues sooner or later," Anna would say to ease Andy's discomfort. "Better she talks about them with people she trusts."

Martin hated Anna's voice.

"No," he said out loud, "I hate *you*, Anna."

She had hardened into something virile, and virulent. A moral zealot, who had probably found Oscar guilty as well, in retrospect, of perversion. What else could she think of a man who had become a tree? Oscar's punishment had been oblivion; Anna had cast his memory into a twilight purgatory, where he would not be mourned or remembered. And now she was influencing Helena.

That's where Helena's gone to, Martin concluded, to Anna's pagan temple by the lake, to sip chilled white wine and exchange unpleasant insights about me, about the burden I am on Helena and her sense of life, how it would be better if she left me, better for me as well. He must learn to live with himself and by himself, he could hear Anna saying. the women around him can no longer be his crutches.

"Anna, don't take her away from me as well," Martin said in a hoarse voice he did not recognise as his own.

He saw himself in Anna's garden, stalking her, and then his hands at her throat. She struggled to breathe, he loved the terror in her eyes, how it gratified him.

Martin awoke from the sleep he had fallen into

on Di's bed, the stench of burning spices in his nostrils. One more thing he hated, he was coherent enough to think: the smell of Indian cooking. He left the house on foot, vaguely aware of how dangerous it was to walk alone through the deserted streets. Thieves and muggers, a devil who'd come to steal his soul? Perils worth risking. He, Martin Wallace, had to rid the world of the evil incarnate in Anna, because only he finally recognised its many insidious and seductive guises.

FATIGYAH HELD a gadat to cleanse the house, at which Imam Ismail chanted "jiekers" in his high-pitched voice. A convocation of bearded young men chorused the Imam's melodic salutations to prophets and saints, fell silent as the Imam's eyes chose one among them to recite verses from "Yasien", the most beautiful of all the Koran's chapters. In the room next door—Malik's old study converted into a comfortable lounge—women joined in spontaneously, their voices rising full-throated for a moment, before falling silent and allowing the men's hoarse voices to hold sway once more. Fatgiyah wept her first tears of real grief for her husband.

Allah maaf, Allah maaf, Fatgiyah prayed, asking God to forgive her for her sins of the mind and the body, mostly desires that made her body ache and her mind tired, asking God to grant

Malik janat, the heavenly peace he deserved, and asking God—the most merciful—to have mercy even on the soul of Amina Mandelstam, whore and murderer. Fatgiyah shut her eyes tight to dispel this discordant thought, and accepted Rabia's hand-wringing sharing of her sorrow. When the gadat was over and their guests had left, Fatgiyah crept into bed. Rabia offered to sleep in her mother's bed for the night, but Fatgiyah gently declined.

"I must get used to its emptiness now."

The affection between mother and daughter had restored itself, this crisis had brought them closer to each other. Fatgiyah fell asleep, secure in the peacefulness of a house filled with the warmth of God's songs, the aroma of sweet "kier" milk, until the anxiety about Fadiel returned to waken her. She lay on her back staring at the ceiling and listening to the rafters which Malik had so ruthlessly silenced beginning to creak, imagining a new silence there, a foreboding absence which their prayers tonight had confirmed.

She longed to call Marianne, to comfort her, soothe her anguish with motherly platitudes, "He'll come back, it's the Khan genes, they have to search, God knows what for . . ." but knew that the efforts would be futile. Marianne's pain was too deep.

She remembered Marianne's bewilderment. "Why, with a woman so much older than him, old

enough to be . . ." Her trailing off had been generous, an attempt not to press deeper the hurt
Fadiel's mother, an older woman, undoubtedly
felt. Fatgiyah's silence had been sharp, like the
intake of knifed breath. When she finally put the
phone down, Marianne had long ago given up
asking, "Are you there, are you there?"

In the hour before dawn, exhaustion finally
brought sleep to Fatgiyah.

ANNA ROSE from her bed and pulled the covers gently over Andy's sprawling body, sealing in
his odours and their warmth, the smell of faded
farts. She smiled at how human she had become,
at least in her tolerance of these inevitable we're-
married-now vulgarities. They endeared him to
her, after all. Di asleep, a peculiar wrinkled peace
in her face. She made tea. Then, warming her
hands around the mug, she sat in the bay window
of her study, carefully avoiding the newspaper
which Martin had smugly dropped on her desk
yesterday, his eyes moving from the paper to
Anna to Di, about to take her quick leave of him
after the dutiful father-daughter trip to the mall.

"So, does little Di understand any of this?" he
asked, then retreated from Anna's angry stare, a
fencer taunting his opponent, knowing that all
she could do was strike at his armour, that her
superiority was hollow, that she dared not go for
his jugular and say, "Did little Di understand

anything when you molested her, did I understand anything?" without wounding herself and her young ward more grievously. Yes, only Martin was capable of this kind of cynicism. "Ugliness? What ugliness?" he might as well have said of his life and his crimes, like a character out of Dostoevsky. What character was that? She could not remember now, could not explain this sudden recollection of something she had read, what, twenty years ago. In any case, her brother Martin was even beyond her despair now.

Anna looked out onto the dark veranda. At the edge of its still darker curve, a wind stirred the dull leaves of autumn. How quickly this would be over and winter here. Long, dry, revealing in all the trees and shrubs a Spartan discretion, an ability to shed all extraneous beauty, to preserve until a more propitious season precious reserves of moisture.

Except for the magnolia. Mug in hand, she stepped out through the study doors—this was her sanctuary, Andy had his and Di hers, though the young girl invaded with such pagan innocence both the other temples of solitude—and appraised the magnolia flowers beginning slowly to enclose themselves and their nocturnal carnality. Anna stopped abruptly. Why did she think of the flower as carnal? Where had she heard this phrase? Not hers at all. It was the sweetness of its smell, that particular emanation of cold semen— she imagined a flower darker than the ones before her, a stench of honey—that brought the tightness to her chest.

Her cry brought Andy stumbling to the veranda, first wrestling with the front door, then running to Anna's study where he knew she often sat reading when she could not sleep. The damp soles of his feet stuck pleasantly to the cool wood, and he relished the sensation, in spite of himself, in spite of his frantic concern for Anna. She's having another asthma attack, he thought, where the hell does it come from?

He found her at the edge of the veranda, staring down into the shadows of the magnolia tree— dark even during the day—her favourite tea-mug clasped to her chest like a crucifix. Martin's body lay there, sprawled, slowly being covered by petals shed from the tree. His throat had been cut—no, ripped, Andy thought, vertically. Some strength that must have taken, no woman could have done it, certainly not Anna, he thought, his defence of her already building up in his mind. Dead some hours, the blood already congealed.

A cold morning, bracing, Andy would say afterwards.

One last flower on the tree thrust out its shameless vulva, until, spurned by Andy's unknowingness, it too closed itself. The beautiful light before the sun came up was long and sharp.

GLOSSARY

AG HERE: Oh God

ALLAH MAAF: request for God's mercy

ALLES-OP-SKOU MEISIES: everything-on-show girls

BALAA: dire trouble

BHAI: literally "brother"; often used derogatorily of Indian men, especially shopkeepers

BOEPENSOUPAS: pot-bellied grandpas

BOEREMEISIE: Afrikaans country girl

BONSELLA: gift; something for free

BULBEFOK DRONK: as drunk as a mad bull

CHARITY SE MOER: dismissive equivalent of "Fuck charity"

CHILI-SMOUS: spice merchant

DIK: satiated, overfull

DINGES: thingumajig

DONDER-EN-BLIKSEM: thunder and lightning

DOOS, DOSIE: cunt

FAH-FEE: Chinese gambling game

FRIS BEVRYDE BOEREMEISIE: fresh (or well-built) liberated country girl

GAMMATJIE: Cape Malay folk figure, a local "Joe Bloggs"

GUJI: Gujarati speaker; often used colloquially to describe meek femininity

HAYI SUKA!: Hey, get away!

HELPMEKAAR: Help-one-another!

HEY, JY MET DIE HONDOEG, WAT KYK JY SOE? JY MOET JOU SUSTER SOE GAAN SIT EN BELOER!: Hey, dog-eye, what are you looking at? Go and leer at your sister!

HOER: whore

INSYPELAAR: infiltrator

IS O'S DAAR?: Are we there?

JAGSE: randy

JANAT: Heaven

JOLLERS: revellers, "party animals"

JOU KLEINE KAK: You little shit!

JURRE: Jeez!

KLONKIE: little boy

KNOP-JOINT: love-nest for a man's mistress

KOEKSISTERS: syrupy Cape Malay confection

KONFYT: fruit preserved in syrup

LANG LANTERN, WEINIG LIG: Tall lantern, little light (used to tease a tall person)

LOER-KOEKELOER: literally "peep-peeping"; voyeuristic

MAGOGO: old woman

MOFFIES: gay men

MOTCHIE: Cape Malay woman

MUTI-MURDERERS: literally "medicine-murderers"; people who kill to obtain body parts for witchcraft

NACASARA: impure; unbeliever

NIKKA: ceremony in which marriage vows are exchanged

NOCH: see, understand

NOG: even

ONNIE: traditional Indian scarf

ONS MENSE BEGRAWE NIE HUL DOOIES ASOF HULLE OP PAD PARTYTJIE TOE IS NIE: Our people don't bury their dead as if they're on their way to a party.

OUMA: Grandma

OUPA: Grandpa

PAMPOENSPREEKWOORDJIES: literally "pumpkin proverbs"; quaint country sayings

PIELE: penises

PIET POMPIES: Joe Soap (with a play on "pomp", fuck)

POEPHOL: arsehole

PONDOKKIES: shacks

ROOIGEVAAR: "red peril"; the threat of communism

RYK-MISTER-KAALGAT: rich mister pauper; a pretentious poor man

SHEG-SLEG: literally "Hajji Bad"; a religious hypocrite

SIES: pathetic, shameful

SKEL: scolding

SKELM: sly

SKOLLIES: rough people (not necessarily thugs)

SKURWE: mangy, dirty

SLAMS, SLAMSE: Muslim; used colloquially to refer to Muslims with Malay ancestry

STILLE: silent

SWART VARK: Black Pig

TIE-TIE: tycoon

TJOEPSTIL: completely silent

VAALIES: disparaging term for people from the Transvaal

VLEI: shallow lake, marshy area

VOETSEK: piss off, go away (usually used to chase a dog)

VOOR-OP-DIE-WA: a forward or presumptuous person; literally "someone at the front of the wagon"

WALAI: colloquial equivalent of "strue's God"

WATSE DING?: Come again?

WIT BOKKIES: white girls

YOU KAK AND YOU KOU: literally "you shit and you chew"; you talk too much.

FICTION/LITERATURE

A *NEW YORK TIMES* NOTABLE BOOK

"ENTIRELY WONDERFUL; MOVING, MYSTERIOUS, WISE
AND PROFOUNDLY PROVOCATIVE."
—*The Baltimore Sun*

HAUNTINGLY LYRICAL and suffused with rich allegory, *Kafka's Curse* — a sensual narrative that unfolds in five magical fables of love, death, politics, and family betrayal — is the extraordinary American debut of the award-winning South African poet Achmat Dangor.

Here is the modern-day story of two brothers: one devoted to apartheid-era assimilation, the other to Islam and tradition. Oscar Kahn (born Omar Khan) is a "colored" Muslim architect passing as a Jewish man and living with his blond wife in the wealthy white suburbs of Johannesburg. For his apostasy, the night following his mother's funeral Omar experiences a mysterious physical metamorphosis, the likes of which no one can explain. As his politician brother, Malik, comes to terms with his brother's betrayal, he abandons both his religious principles and his family as he falls in love with Amina, Omar's beautiful psychotherapist. Brilliantly conceived and powerfully evoked, *Kafka's Curse* is an imaginative reinterpretation of an Arabic fairy tale and announces the arrival of Achmat Dangor at the forefront of contemporary literature.

"I have rarely read anything in prose that is at once so dense and so bright. *Kafka's Curse* opens like a music box to a shiny intricate machinery and a sweet precise music, and it closes on a note of hope that can only cheer observers of South Africa's recent transformation." —*Boston Book Review*

"Immensely enjoyable. Dangor's prose [has] lyrical energy and freshness....This is a South Africa you haven't encountered in fiction before." —Nadine Gordimer

U.S. $12.00 / CAN. $17.95

ISBN 0-375-70462-0

COVER DESIGN:
EVAN GAFFNEY DESIGN
COVER PHOTOGRAPHS:
TOP, BINDER & WALSH / PHOTONICA;
BOTTOM, HAMID SOJNAR / PHOTONICA

51200

9 780375 704628

VINTAGE INTERNATIONAL   www.vintagebooks.com